KEITH CALABRESE

WILD RIDE

ALSO BY KEITH CALABRESE

Connect the Dots

A Drop of Hope

WILD RIDE

KEITH CALABRESE

SCHOLASTIC PRESS / NEW YORK

Names: Calabrese, Keith, author.
Title: Wild Ride / Keith Calabrese.
Description: First edition. | New York: Scholastic Press, 2022. | Audience: Ages 8–12. | Audience: Grades 7–9. | Summary: Seventh grader Charley Decker's mother is on vacation with her boyfriend, and Charley plans to spend the weekend watching movies with her best friends Wade and Oona and her older brother, Greg; but Greg has a date and takes their mother's boyfriend's expensive, rare automobile, then manages to get it towed; Charley and her friends hatch a plan to get the car back—but things go seriously wrong when they discover somebody called Mitch hiding from a pair of scary dudes in the trunk of the car, and the three friends find themselves on the wildest ride of their lives.
Identifiers: LCCN 2021021946 (print) | LCCN 2021021947 (ebook) | ISBN 9781338743241 (hardcover) | ISBN 9781338797756 (ebook)
Subjects: LCSH: Antique and classic cars—Juvenile fiction. | Criminals—Juvenile fiction. | Escapes—Juvenile fiction. | Rescues—Juvenile fiction. | Best friends—Juvenile fiction. | Brothers and sisters—Juvenile fiction. | Adventure stories. | Humorous stories. | CYAC: Automobiles—Fiction. | Criminals—Fiction. | Escapes—Fiction. | Rescues—Fiction. | Friendship—Fiction. | Brothers and sisters—Fiction. | Adventure and adventurers—Fiction. | Humorous stories. | BISAC: JUVENILE FICTION / Action & Adventure / General | JUVENILE FICTION / Humorous Stories | LCGFT: Action and adventure fiction. | Humorous fiction.
Classification: LCC PZ7.1.C276 Wi 2022 (print) | LCC PZ7.1.C276 (ebook) | DDC 813.6 [Fic]—dc23
LC record available at https://lccn.loc.gov/2021021946
LC ebook record available at https://lccn.loc.gov/2021021947

10 9 8 7 6 5 4 3 2 1   22 23 24 25 26

Printed in Italy   183

First printing, February 2022

Book design by Stephanie Yang

For Alison

The following redacted interview is the only surviving document related to a series of highly classified events that have been dubbed informally (and somewhat amusingly) by the Senate Intelligence Committee as "The Mustang Redundancy."

Department of Justice
Federal Bureau
of Investigations

Witness Interview: ██████ ██████

Transcript

April 17, ████

8:18 a.m.

[Interview of subject conducted by Special Agent Karen Hill and Special Agent Allen Dale]

[Subject, ██████ ██████, is female, 12 years of age, and will herein be referred to as "Witness 2"]

Special Agent Hill: You have to admit, it's a pretty incredible story.

Witness 2: Oh, I know. Ma'am.

Special Agent Hill: And by incredible, I'm using the "difficult to believe" definition of the term.

Witness 2: Yeah. I got that. Look, where's my brother? And where's ███?

Special Agent Hill: I believe I'm asking the questions, young lady.

Witness 2: Look, I've already told you everything. Twice. What more could you possibly need to know?

Special Agent Dale: Doughnut?

Witness 2: Huh?

Special Agent Dale: Want a doughnut?

Special Agent Hill: Seriously, Allen?

Special Agent Dale: What? The kid looks scared.

Witness 2: I'm not scared.

Special Agent Dale: I could look for one with sprinkles. Might help, like, cut the tension.

Special Agent Hill: Shut up, Allen.

Witness 2: I don't want a doughnut. I just want to see my brother and ███.

Special Agent Hill: Then explain to me what the three of you were doing with two known felons like ███ and ███ ████████?

Witness 2: Doing? They kidnapped us!

4

Special Agent Hill: I thought you said they kidnapped ██████████ .

Witness 2: Well, yeah. They did. But that was before.

Special Agent Hill: At the restaurant?

Witness 2: ██ █████████ , yeah.

Special Agent Hill: Where you met the ████████████ brothers?

Witness 2: No.

Special Agent Dale: Aha! Where you met ████████████ !

Witness 2: No! Like I said, we didn't meet anyone at ██ █████████ . We just went there for burgers and milk-shakes. All this other stuff just sort of happened.

Special Agent Hill: See, that's where you lose me. So, the ██████████████ brothers just happened to pick your car to ██ ██ █████████ ████ █ ████ ██ ████ ██ ███ .

Witness 2: They didn't know it was our car! They thought it was ████ █████ car.

Special Agent Hill: To be clear, you are referring to tech billionaire ████ ███ ?

Witness 2: Yes! For the last time, that's the guy! Like I said, the ██████████████ brothers work for him. Look, you're wasting time. You need to find him. Now.

Special Agent Hill: Take it easy.

Witness 2: No! I won't take it easy. Haven't you been listening to me at all? This guy is really dangerous. To everyone. What part of that isn't sinking into those thick skulls of yours?

Special Agent Dale: [inaudible noise, possibly a snicker]

Special Agent Hill: You know, young lady, you have a serious mouth on you. Anyone ever tell you that?

Witness 2: Once or twice. That doughnut still on the table?

Special Agent Dale: Sure. Sprinkles or jelly?

Special Agent Hill: Sit down, Allen. Okay, ████. Let's try this again. From the beginning.

According to the United States government,

what you are about to read never happened . . .

ONE

On Friday afternoon, shortly before the final bell, Charley Decker received detention for mouthing off to her teacher. Charley didn't get in trouble much. It kind of caught everyone by surprise.

Wade was waiting for her when she finally got out. He was trying not to smirk, but he wasn't trying very hard.

"Don't start," Charley said.

"At least Mr. Bonino didn't keep you that long," Wade offered.

"He shouldn't have kept me at all," Charley protested.

Wade shrugged.

"What?"

"Charley, seriously," Wade said. "You kind of asked for it."

"What part of 'don't start' aren't you getting?"

9

"Fine," Wade said, dropping it. "See any familiar faces in the big house?"

"Parker Nadal was in there, too. I don't know what for."

"I do," Wade chuckled.

"Really? Who was he impersonating this time?"

"Not 'who,'" Wade corrected. "'What.' Remember the T. rex from *Jurassic Park*?"

"Sure," Charley said. "Wait. He didn't!"

"He did. During passing period. You could hear it all the way down B Hall."

"No way," Charley laughed. "Was it good?"

"Good enough to make a bunch of sixth graders cry."

"He does have a gift."

"Yeah," Wade agreed. "But hey, you mouthed off to the nicest teacher in school. Now that's hard-core."

Charley gave him a look but couldn't hold it for long. Everybody needs at least one friend who has no qualms about telling you when you're full of it. Charley had long ago realized that Wade Harris would always be that friend for her. She just wished he wasn't so good at it.

"It isn't a bad word," she huffed defiantly.

"Sure."

Charley said, "Just don't say anything in front of Greg, okay?"

"'Course," Wade said as they started walking home. "We still on, then, for New Farouk's and everything?"

"You bet," Charley said, brightening a bit. "Greg promised."

Greg was Charley's older brother. It was more than that, though. They were pals, always had been. There were five and a half years between them—Greg was eighteen and she was twelve—but he never treated her like it. He treated her more like his partner in crime. He was always there when she needed him, always had her back.

This year, though, everything was changing. Greg was a senior in high school, and soon he'd be going off to college. Charley was already starting to miss him. Greg wasn't around the house much anymore. Lately, he was always out with his friends, or at baseball practice, or with Marisa.

Mostly with Marisa.

And even when Greg was around, Marisa was usually there, too. They'd been dating all year and Greg was still totally moony for her. She even came to family game night. It was bad enough when their mom's boyfriend, Derrick, had started showing up. Now game night was practically a couples' thing. What was the point anymore?

Take two weeks ago. They were playing Scrabble—Charley, Greg, Mom, and Derrick. Marisa wasn't there, but she may as well have been because Greg was texting her, like, every two minutes. Anyway, it was Charley's turn and she had two *f*'s, an *a*, a *d*, a *t*, an *i*, and an *r*. She used them all, a natural bingo (and a double word score to boot, but who's counting), and did Greg even notice? Please, he barely looked up from his phone.

Everything was changing.

For the last week it had just been the two of them in the house. Their mom and Derrick were in Hawaii for vacation, but they'd be getting back tomorrow. At first Charley had been looking forward to this week, just her and her brother. She'd hoped it would give them a chance to hang out like they used to. But it wasn't working out that way.

One way or another, her brother always seemed to be out the door. He and Marisa had been off doing stuff together every day since Mom and Derrick left. They were always *busy*. Always on the go. Charley got to tag along sometimes, to watch Marisa's track meet, or Greg's doubleheader. Whoopee. Like that counted.

And even when Greg was around, he wasn't *there*, not really. Hanging out at home made him all twitchy and distracted. Like he was trapped, or grounded. And he barely noticed Charley anymore, even when they were in the same room together.

But tonight was going to be different. Charley was going to make sure of it. Greg had promised to take her and Wade to New

Farouk's for burgers and shakes. The diner's full name was New Farouk's Famous Ice Cream and Brazier, and they made the best milkshakes in Chicago. The burgers were good, too, but it was really all about the milkshakes. At least that's what Charley thought. It was her favorite place to eat, and the kind of hang-out thing Charley had hoped they'd be doing all week.

Then, after New Farouk's, the three of them would come back to the house and watch their favorite movies all night, just like they used to do when Greg was in middle school and Charley and Wade were just in grade school. The coolest movies. Movies they had been too young to watch. That's what made Greg such an awesome big brother. Like *Purple Rain* and the first two *Alien* movies—but you had to stop after that—and *Galaxy Quest* and *Hot Fuzz.*

Charley had the whole night planned out. Tonight was going to be like old times. Like it used to be. Tonight was going to be the best.

Wade and Charley walked through the garage on their way into Charley's house. They came in the side door and Charley dropped her bag on the kitchen island. Wade lingered behind in the doorway.

"Man," Wade said, gazing adoringly at Derrick's Mustang. "That is some car."

"You say that every time."

"It bears repeating. Every time."

Greg was upstairs; it sounded like he was on the phone.

"You still good to stay over?" Charley asked.

"No problem," Wade said as he joined her at the island. "It's a gap weekend."

Wade's parents were divorced. They were also both lawyers. They shared Wade through a joint-custody agreement that was so complicated it required a computer algorithm to enforce.

But with all the back-and-forth, there were bound to be gaps. Misread emails, blind spots in the code. Days when neither Wade's mother nor father technically had custody of Wade. But since his parents never actually talked to each other, no one really noticed.

The first time it happened, Wade hadn't said anything. He'd just gone to stay with his uncle Terry in the city and waited for someone—his parents, their lawyers, the algorithm—to figure out the mistake.

That was two years ago.

Wade didn't mind much. He always had a blast with his uncle Terry. Besides, no one had ever asked him whether he wanted a stupid computer program to tell him where to eat and sleep and do his homework. So why should he help his parents micro-manage *his* life?

Greg came downstairs. He was still in his baseball clothes, talking excitedly on his cell phone.

"No, no," he said. "I want to wait and surprise Mom and Derrick when they get back tomorrow. Yeah. Okay, see you soon." He ended the call and put the phone back in his pocket.

"Hey, you're home," he said, noticing Charley and Wade. "Where were you guys? It's later than usual."

"Loitering," Charley said.

"Light trespassing," Wade added.

"How was practice?" Charley asked, to get them off the subject.

"Aw, fine. Coach let us out early on account of yesterday's doubleheader. Never mind that, though. Guess what." His eyes looked big, like he'd just pounded two iced coffees.

"What?" Charley asked warily.

He held up his phone. "I just found out ... I got into the University of British Columbia!"

Charley felt like somebody had just knocked the wind out of her. "In Canada?" she managed.

"Hey, that's great," Wade said, reading the acceptance email on Greg's phone. "Congratulations!"

"Thanks! It's my first choice. I'm so stoked."

Wade sat down on one of the stools while Greg gushed about how excellent UBC was going to be. Charley sat, too, but she didn't say anything. She hadn't known he was looking at schools that were thousands of miles away. She stared into space for a good ten minutes while the boys prattled on until she heard her brother say to Wade, "So, you're coming with us to New Farouk's?"

"Yeah. If that's cool."

"Absolutely," Greg said. "We need to celebrate, right?" He looked over at his sister. "Charley?"

"Huh?"

"New Farouk's? Still want to go?"

"Definitely," Charley said, perking up a little.

"Great! Let me shower and get changed. Then as soon as Marisa gets here, we'll head out."

"Great," Charley said. Then: "Wait, what?"

TWO

"Marisa," Greg said with that goofy look he got whenever the very concept of his girlfriend was broached. "She's on her way."

Charley couldn't believe it. She'd made it pretty clear it was supposed to be just the three of them tonight. Of course, she didn't exactly say "no Marisa," but anyone with half a brain would have taken the hint. That was it, though. When it came to Marisa, Greg didn't have half a brain. All he had were glands.

Greg showered, changed, and was back downstairs in ten minutes flat. As if on cue, the doorbell rang.

"And there she is," Greg said, bounding for the front door like a golden retriever with acute separation anxiety.

Charley gritted her teeth. "Perfect."

She was, too. Perfect. Perfect Marisa Ng. She was tall and

17

smart and funny and graceful. Worst of all, she was cool. Marisa could get along with anybody. Even Charley, who didn't make it easy.

And, of course, she was pretty. Scratch that, beautiful. Dangerously beautiful. As in Greg could hardly keep his eyes on the road whenever they all drove somewhere.

Even Wade got all googly around her. He'd get this *crushing on the babysitter* look on his face while he tried to make his voice sound deeper.

"What?" Wade said defensively, when Charley gave him a disgusted look for doing just that after Marisa glided into the kitchen.

"Hey, Charley," Marisa said warmly. "So, what do we think about this British Columbia business?"

"It's far," Charley said.

"I bet when he comes back for Thanksgiving, he'll have already forgotten how to pronounce his *o*'s."

Wade and Marisa laughed. Charley rolled her eyes.

"Actually," Greg said, "the accent is a lot less pronounced in Vancouver."

"We'll see *aboot* that," Wade chimed in.

"Ha!" Greg said. "Good one."

"Hey, I'm starving," Marisa cut in. "You guys ready to go?"

"Absolutely," Greg said, grabbing a set of keys from the bowl on the counter. "But what do you say we go . . . in style."

"The Mustang?" Wade whispered, as if it were a word of great mystical power.

"It's a celebration, right?"

"Are you sure?" Marisa asked hesitantly. Charley was with her brother's girlfriend on this one. Derrick was a pretty chill guy, but the one thing he'd said before he and their mom had left for the airport was *don't* drive the Mustang. He was pretty serious about it.

"Derrick's let me drive it before."

"With *him*," Charley added.

"It'll be fine," Greg said, already heading for the side door to the garage.

An uneasy feeling told Charley that it wouldn't be, and that she should say so. But it was followed by another feeling that told her not to say anything. That it wasn't her problem.

Charley listened to the wrong one.

Derrick's car was a Mustang convertible. But not just *any* Mustang convertible. It was a Raven Black 1964 World's Fair Skyway Mustang. They'd only made, like, twelve of them. Total.

The Skyway Mustangs were the centerpiece of the Ford pavilion at the 1964 World's Fair in New York. People waited for hours just to sit in the cars, which rode on tracks through "The Magic Skyway," a massive attraction designed by the people who made Disneyland, with exhibits that started with dinosaurs and went all the way into the future. It was kind of like the "It's a Small World" ride, except cool because you were in a Mustang instead of a little kiddie boat.

Derrick loved this car. His uncle had left it to him or something. He always wanted to put the top down and take them all for a spin. Sometimes they didn't even go anywhere, they just drove. Charley didn't get it. On weekends, Derrick and Greg would set up the Bluetooth speakers on the patio and spend a whole Saturday afternoon washing and waxing it. Derrick took an entire month teaching Greg how to drive stick on this car. It was his prized possession.

Wade broke the revered silence.

"That is some car."

Greg looked at Wade, his eyes full to the brim with mischief and delight. "Get in."

Wade was so excited he actually squeaked a little as he climbed in the back. Charley got in on the other side. She did not squeak.

"Okay," Greg said as the Mustang rumbled ferociously to life. "Let the fun begin."

At least he's driving better, Charley thought.

Greg's hands were locked tightly at ten and two on the steering wheel. Marisa rode shotgun, naturally, but Charley's brother barely turned his head all the way from their house in Evanston to New Farouk's on the Northwest Side of Chicago.

Seeing as they were in a convertible and spring was in the air, Greg drove north a little first, up to the Bahá'í temple, so they could take Sheridan Road back down through the Northwestern campus. It was a beautiful evening. Charley glanced across the back seat at Wade, who, with the wind in his hair and setting sun on his face, was soaking up every second of it.

Charley usually liked driving down Sheridan like this. Northwestern was pretty. But today it just reminded her of how Greg would soon be leaving home for another college like this one, far away. In Canada.

Once they were through campus, Sheridan hugged Lake Michigan all the way until it turned into Lake Shore Drive. Charley now had the water on her left, and the Chicago skyline straight ahead. Two killer views, but she wasn't feeling either of them.

Meanwhile, she was fielding a barrage of texts from Oona.

Fifteen in the last five minutes, and each as long as Charley's arm. If Wade was the friend who told Charley when she was full of it, then Oona Adair was the friend who told her everything else. They'd met last year when they sat next to each other in sixth grade science class. Oona was always objecting to the way Mr. Mathis taught the human development unit.

"I take your point, Oona," the poor, haggard man had said so many times he probably still muttered the words in his sleep, "but state guidelines strictly prohibit me from expounding further on the subject."

That was pretty much Oona in a nutshell—frequently right, invariably exhausting. She was . . . a lot. Charley couldn't even bring herself to read everything her friend was ranting about right now. She skimmed through the texts and picked up something about Oona's clueless parents, the evils of capitalism, and the naked aggression of modern technology. Or maybe it was the naked aggression of capitalism and the evils of modern technology. Oona did have a way with words—there were just so many of them.

Greg took the Montrose exit off Lake Shore Drive and headed

west, approaching the massive corporate headquarters for Pangea, the global retail-tech-social media giant. An animated graphic of the continents rejoining into one landmass flashed across the huge digital billboard over the building's entrance, followed by the company's tagline BRINGING THE WORLD TOGETHER—AGAIN!

The billboard then switched to an ad teasing the arrival of the new Pangea Ursula. It featured a black obelisk floating in a sea of white over the caption RELAX. LET URSULA DO THAT FOR YOU.

Greg pulled into New Farouk's and found a spot in back of the lot next to a Pangea delivery van. Charley's sour mood was not improved when, on the way into the restaurant, she was nearly knocked to the ground by someone coming out.

"Oh, sorry," the guy said in a slow, almost underwater voice as Charley fixed him with her BFC (Burn, Foul Creature) glare. He was a young guy, midtwenties, slight, and very agitated. Clipped onto the pocket of his oxford shirt was a Pangea ID tag with his name and picture.

Charley regained her footing and was about to give the clumsy jerk a word or two, but the abject terror and confusion on his face gave her pause. Charley's BFC face had that effect sometimes.

"I'm real...verrrry..." the guy trailed off as he stumbled away from the restaurant.

Charley and Wade tried to get through the door again, but this time she was brushed back by two burly men in flannels and blue jeans who barreled past her on their way out as well.

"Hey!" she yelled in protest, but it was like they didn't even know, much less care, that she was there.

Wade shrugged. "Maybe the universe is trying to tell you something."

"That I may as well be invisible? Message received."

Wade laughed. "Let me try." He opened the door with exaggerated caution, poking his head inside to see if the coast was, indeed, clear. "Okay, I think we're good."

It was already crowded inside the restaurant and they had to wait a few minutes at the check-in stand.

Greg gave Charley a little nudge. "Wanna play the line game?"

"Ooh," Marisa said, intrigued. "Do it, you guys. I've been dying to see this."

Charley gave Marisa a surprised look, then shook her head. "It's too loud," she said.

The hostess found them four stools at the counter. Charley and Greg took the middle seats, with Wade on the other side of Charley, and Marisa on the other side of Greg.

"So," Marisa said a while later, trying to get a conversation going. "When does your mom get back?"

"They're flying out tonight," Greg said. "Red-eye into San Francisco, then connecting to Chicago. They land at O'Hare tomorrow afternoon around four thirty."

"How long have she and Derrick been together anyway?" Wade chimed in.

Charley shrugged. Greg said, "About a year, I guess."

"Interesting," Marisa said with a somewhat mischievous look as a waitress slid their plates onto the counter.

"What do you mean?" Greg said, clueless as usual.

"Well, you know. Vacation in Hawaii, just the two of them . . ." Marisa let it hang there. Greg and Wade both looked at her blankly. They didn't get it, but Charley did. She'd been thinking the same thing all week. Long courtship—or whatever old people like her mom and Derrick called it—plus romantic island vacation usually equaled engagement. For all Charley knew, Derrick was proposing to her mom right now, on top of a volcano or something.

But then, why would it be on Greg's radar? He'd be leaving home in a few months, for Canada no less. If Mom and Derrick got married, it wouldn't really affect him that much. Besides, he and Derrick were all buddy-buddy. He probably couldn't wait to start calling him "Dad."

Marisa saw the look on Charley's face, dropped the matter with a quick "Never mind," and turned her attention to her veggie burger.

"Dude," Wade said to Charley a few minutes later, when Greg and Marisa were engaged in their own, side conversation. "Are you going to be like this all night?"

"Maybe," Charley said matter-of-factly. "Did you hear her? She knows about the line game."

"What?"

"Marisa. Greg told her about the line game."

"So? You've told me about the line game."

Charley scoffed. "You don't count."

"Thanks?"

Charley resumed sulking over her cheeseburger.

Wade let out a big sigh. "Look, the way I see it, you've got two choices. You can keep scowling into your milkshake, shooting your BFC look at anyone who even tries to talk to you—"

"Good. I think I'll stick with that—"

"Or maybe you can be a little flexible for a change."

"For a change?"

"Yeah. For a change. You ever heard the expression that fifty percent of something is better than one hundred percent of nothing?"

Charley huffed and folded her arms. Wade took her silence for assent. "We're at New Farouk's, Charley. Hamburgers and milkshakes, your favorite! And there's a movie marathon waiting when we get back to your house. So what if your brother's girlfriend tags along? We can still make this an awesome night. Right?"

Charley shrugged.

"Good. Now drink your milkshake." He gave her a little shoulder check. "And maybe try to smile more."

She gave one back, harder. Wade rolled with it.

"You'd be so much prettier if you smiled more." He struggled to keep a straight face.

"Jerk." She laughed, finally breaking.

Then Charley started to get another blast of texts on her phone.

"Oona freaking out again?"

Charley nodded as she skimmed along. "She's been worked up all afternoon."

"Shocker," Wade said. "What is it this time?"

Charley wasn't exactly sure. She put the phone on the counter for him to see as well.

6:25

They're fools!

6:25

Fools, Charley! Nothing but mindless, bourgeois Vichy capitalist fools.

6:25

Slaves to the tech-overlord Alton Peck.

"Alton Peck?" Wade said. "The Pangea guy? What's her beef with him?"

Quite a lot, according to the ongoing flurry of texts.

6:26

But do they even care?

6:26

Of course, they don't!

6:26

Because they don't want to.

6:26

Nobody wants to.

6:27

Because everybody *loves* Pangea. It makes everything so easy. It's soooo convenient. Never mind that Alton Peck is using it to completely rob humanity of its collective free will. No biggie.

6:27

Not as long as they can buy, buy, buy like lab rats pushing the water button. As long as they keep getting their retail food pellets, why rock the boat?

"Okay, I'm lost," Wade said. "Who are the lab rats?"

"Her parents, I think."

"And what did they even do exactly?"

Charley honestly had no idea. When Oona got especially worked up, she tended to write in a frantic, over-caffeinated kind of stream of consciousness that was not easy to follow.

The phone lit up with another blast of texts.

6:28

Corporate malfeasance?

6:28

Add to cart.

6:28

Worker mistreatment, global price fixing, municipal extortion?

6:28

Add to cart.

6:28

Add to cart.

6:28

Add to cardamon.

"Cardamon?"

"Hold on," Charley said.

6:29

*cart

"Ah," Wade said. "I still don't get it, though. I mean, do you?" he asked.

"Kind of?" Charley said, slowing down to reread the text chain more carefully. It didn't help. Oona had a habit of losing the argumentative forest through the trees of her rage, and until she'd had a dozen or so cleansing breaths, there was no pinning her down to specifics.

6:30

Charley, you get that this is serious, right?

6:30

Why aren't you responding?

6:31

Oh, goddess.

6:31

> You aren't with *him*, are you?

"Is she talking about me?" Wade asked defensively.

"No," Charley said, a few seconds too late.

6:32

> You are, aren't you?

6:32

> Seriously. Why do you even bother with that guy?

6:32

> Look, just give him something shiny to play with and text me back.

"She *is* talking about me!"

Charley snatched the phone off the counter.

"Seriously, Charley. What is her deal?" He was asking in a general sense, but Charley knew he also meant it in a more specific, personal way. He and Oona had always gotten along okay, but they weren't tight, not by any means. They were friendly, for Charley's sake, but not friends. If it weren't for Charley, they'd probably never interact.

Lately, though, Oona had been treating Wade with a pointed frostiness that was getting harder to overlook. Little jabs under her breath, pretending Wade wasn't there when he talked, that sort of thing. Wade, for his part, seemed more perplexed than hurt by the obvious change in climate. He'd been letting it all go, so far, but Charley got the feeling that wasn't going to last much longer.

"She does this sometimes," Charley said, putting her phone back in her pocket as Greg settled the check.

There was less traffic on the way north back to Evanston. The Mustang, naturally, didn't have Bluetooth or an aux cord, but Marisa found a classic rock station on the car radio, and soon the four of them were all singing loudly in the open convertible on their way up the waterfront.

Maybe Wade is right, Charley thought. *Maybe the night won't be a total waste after all.*

THREE

"You're what?!"

"We're . . . going out," Greg said, fidgeting awkwardly. "Me and Marisa."

They were back home, standing in the driveway. Charley and Wade had made it to the front door before they realized that Greg and Marisa weren't following them inside.

Charley glared at her brother. "You're serious," she said.

"Well, yeah," Greg said weakly. He was acting all restless and antsy again. Like he'd already put in enough time with Charley and couldn't wait to get out of there.

"I thought we were watching movies," Charley said, trying to hide the hurt in her voice.

"We can still do that later. We're only going out for a

while. I'm dropping Marisa at Stacey's around midnight."

"Midnight?"

"One o'clock at the latest. Tell you what, you and Wade get started and then when I come home, we can stay up all night and finish. I'll even pick up some doughnuts for a midnight snack."

"Don't you mean a one o'clock snack?" Charley said dryly.

"Charley . . ." he pleaded. His tone said *be reasonable*, but she could see his gaze already drifting down the driveway.

"Whatever," Charley said as she keyed open the front door. "Where are you guys even going?"

"Into the city," he said, taking the bait. "There's this jazz spot near Loyola—"

"Have fun," Charley interrupted, slamming the front door before her brother could finish.

Charley plopped down on the couch and pouted. She would bristle at such a childlike term, but seeing as how she kept sinking deeper into the cushions with her arms folded, her bottom lip out, and her eyebrows as low as they could go without squinting, there really wasn't a better word for it.

"We could go out, too," Wade said eventually. It had been about twenty minutes since Greg and Marisa had left. They had put one of the movies on, but neither one was really watching it.

"Oh, yeah? Where?"

"We could go to Sassy's."

Charley chuckled. "Sure, we could."

"I'm serious. Well, mostly serious. But hey, I'm game if it would cheer you up."

Charley seriously considered the offer. She had always been extremely curious about his uncle Terry's cabaret; Wade had been telling her stories about the place for years. Then the doorbell rang. Wade gave her a curious look as Charley shrugged and went to answer it.

"And so, finally, it came to this. The family she loved, forsaken her. The only home she knew, home no more. But it was the only way. Things were said, truths revealed. Horrible truths that could not be undone, chasms of principle that could never be breached. Now all she could do was make her own way in the world. The scales finally fallen from her eyes. Forever."

Charley looked at the girl standing on the threshold of the front door, talking rapidly into her phone.

"Hey there, Oona."

"Charley, thank the goddess you're here," Oona said, putting her phone in her pocket before wrapping Charley in a desperate hug. Then, taking her friend by the shoulders to brace her for what was next, she looked Charley mournfully in the eyes and added: "I've done it. I've run away from home."

A couple of things about Oona. The first was that she wanted to be a writer, so to practice she liked to narrate her life in real time, into the recording app on her phone. Which is what she'd been doing when Charley opened the front door.

Charley was used to this. She was also used to Oona running away from home. That was the other thing. Well, part of it anyway. Oona ran away from her parents every four to six weeks, always following some big blowout argument. But, invariably, it was Oona doing all the blowing out. Oona's parents were sweet, soft-spoken people who only ever wanted to nurture and support their daughter, but spent a lot of time just trying to figure out what she was yelling about.

Basically, Oona was hardwired to challenge authority and stand up to the forces of tyranny. Unfortunately for Oona, she was woefully lacking in any actual day-to-day tyranny. She desperately wanted to fight the power, but that was hard to do when the power only asked if you were getting enough sleep or wanted a juice box.

The good news was that since Oona's fights with her parents were always so innocuous and one-sided, they generally blew over pretty quickly. In fact, she'd run away so many times that her parents didn't even bother calling Charley anymore to make sure that's where their daughter was. They just tracked her on her phone, made sure she was safe and sound at her friend's house, and waited patiently for the storm to pass and Oona to announce that she was "open to reconciliation."

"It's for *real* this time," Oona said with a defeated sigh as she followed Charley into the house. "I absolutely *can't* go back."

"Uh-huh," Charley said.

Oona dropped her overnight bag on the kitchen counter. She was about to go on, but then she spotted Wade coming in from the family room. "Oh," she said.

"Hey, Oona."

"Hello, Wade," she said with the arctic blast of an English butler who just spied you eating your dinner with the salad fork.

"What happened?" Charley asked.

"What?"

"Your parents. Why are you running away?"

"Didn't you get all my texts?"

"Well, yeah. But, to be honest, they were kind of hard to follow. I mean, one minute your parents are lab rats, then somehow Alton Peck is in there . . ."

"Charley!" Oona exclaimed. "They gave me an Ursula! An *Ursula!*"

"No way!" Wade exclaimed. "That's awesome!"

"It certainly isn't."

"What are you talking about? I'd kill for one of those."

"Whoa, whoa," Charley interjected. "Hold on a minute. Who, or what, is an Ursula?"

Wade and Oona both gave Charley the *have-you-been-living-under-a-rock* look, then Wade pulled up a teaser ad on his phone.

The short answer, technologically speaking, was that an Ursula was, pretty much, everything. A thin, two-foot-tall black obelisk, the Pangea Ursula was an artificially intelligent device, a digital life assistant that responded to voice commands, answered questions, and did just about anything short of buttering your bread. The Ursula was also a computer that could digitally project all sorts of 3D computer graphics, like a keyboard or virtual desktop, or display emails and even videos. It fulfilled every technical need a person could have, and it took up as much space as a paperweight.

"It looks like the thing from *2001*," Charley said when the video ended.

"Ha," Wade chuckled. "It does."

"You guys," Oona huffed. "This is *serious*."

"I wonder if it can talk to you in a British accent," Charley mused.

"You mean like *Iron Man*? Oh, it can," Wade said. "But they're impossible to get. They don't even go on sale to the public until Monday."

"I know," Oona huffed again. "Because Pangea isn't finished blanketing the planet with their armada of Ursula satellites yet. You know how many they've launched already?"

"No. Don't care. So, wait. How'd you get one?"

"Alton Peck is giving them out early to Pangea employees. My dad's marketing firm does some work for them," Oona said, her eyes downcast in shame.

"Sweet."

"No, Wade. It is not *sweet*. Or *awesome*. Those things are *insidious*. They're just one more way for Alton Peck and Pangea to infiltrate and control our every waking moment. I mean, any fool can see that."

"Oh, really?"

Charley could feel the tension in the room ramping up by the second. "Guys . . ."

"Your parents give you the hottest new tech on the planet and your response is to run away from home. Yeah, sure. I'm the fool."

"Yes, Wade. You are."

"That's rich," Wade said. Then added: "And, yes. Pun intended."

"That's enough!" Charley bellowed.

A long silence followed as both Wade and Oona wisely followed the old "if you can't say something nice" maxim.

The silence was broken by Charley's cell phone. It was her brother, Greg.

"Oh, what now?" she growled as she answered the phone. "Yeah? Huh? Slow down. Greg, I can't . . . what do you mean . . . didn't see what sign?"

Wade and Oona leaned closer to Charley as she talked to her brother on the phone. Their shared curiosity was the only thing they'd agreed on since Oona had arrived.

Charley listened for a bit, then blurted out, "You lost the car?!"

"The Mustang?!" Wade shrieked, grabbing Charley's arm with the level of panic generally reserved for a toddler who has just wandered onto a construction site. "Greg lost the Skyway?!"

She shook her head dismissively. "Towed," she said.

"Oh, thank god."

"Four hundred dollars?" she screeched incredulously into her phone. "That seems really high. Uh-huh. Uh-huh. What do they mean it's 'down'?" She went to a drawer and pulled out an envelope of money. "Okay, there's about a hundred and forty left here. How much do you have on you? Uh-huh."

Oona pulled a wad of bills out of her pocket. "Tell him I've got sixty-seven. Oh, and my CTA TAP card."

"Maybe we can barter for the difference," Wade suggested. "Oona, look up what the street value is on a Pangea Ursula."

"Very funny."

"Shut up, will you?" Charley snapped at her friends. "The connection is garbage. No, not you, Greg. Look, don't worry, you can borrow my babysitting money. Tell me where you are and I'll bring—no, that's okay. She doesn't have to . . . no, Greg, really . . ." She put down her phone, looked at her friends, and sighed, "You're not going to believe this."

"What's going on?" Oona said. "Is Greg all right?"

"He's fine," Charley said, then filled them in on the rest. Greg and Marisa were presently at the impound lot where the Mustang was towed, but the lot owner wanted four hundred bucks to get the car back.

"Can't they just put it on a credit card?"

"Machine's down, apparently. So it has to be cash. Greg and Marisa only have sixty on them, but we still have a little bit of the money our mom left us for food, and I can cover the rest."

"That's great," Oona said. "But how do we get the money to them?"

"Marisa's on her way," Charley said, with a bit of a scowl.

"She's taking an Uber here, then she'll drive her car back to the impound lot with the money."

"Perfect!" Oona said.

Charley thought for a minute. "You know, maybe it is."

"Charley," Wade said, following her out of her bedroom while she counted out her babysitting money. "This isn't a good idea."

"Look, I'm just trying to help. Why shouldn't I come along?"

Wade wasn't buying it. He knew that look on her face.

"What?" Charley said defensively. She knew the look on Wade's face, too. "If you think about it, my butt's on the line here, too. If we don't get the Mustang back before my mom and Derrick come home—"

"C'mon. That's not why you want to go," Wade said as they returned to the kitchen, where Oona was sitting at the island, drinking a soda, and narrating into her phone.

"*Like all men, Wade was accustomed to telling women what they were really thinking.*"

"What? Hey, stop that."

"*Perhaps sensing that his alpha male posturing would have no effect on the likes of Charley Decker, the boy backpedaled in his*

Vans and decided to direct his hostilities to the other woman in the room."

"Is she going to do that all night?"

". . . he asked, a faint warble of fear in his voice. Or was that just puberty?"

"Probably," Charley said, amused.

"Whatever. I'm just saying, for the record: This night is not going to go like you think it will."

"Noted," Charley said. "You're still coming, though, aren't you?"

"Oh, yeah. Definitely. I absolutely intend to say 'I told you' so in real time."

=o===o=

"She moved with an easy grace that was both powerful and elegant. Though Oona had met her once or twice before, it was only upon seeing her now, lit from below by the pathway lights leading from the driveway to the house, that she realized how goddesslike Marisa Ng really was. She may even have been, if such a thing were actually possible for a woman, almost too perfect."

"Oona," Charley said testily as they watched Marisa get out of the Uber, say goodbye to the driver, and make her way up the walk.

"Perhaps that was why Charley insisted on bringing the money to Greg herself. Anyone as exceptional as Marisa had to be harboring some kind of hidden issues. Maybe, *Charley wondered, she was a kleptomaniac."*

"She's not a klepto—"

"Charley protested. Nevertheless, Marisa was clearly out of Greg's league, which was perhaps why Charley had always been suspicious of her."

The doorbell rang.

"I'm not suspicious of her. I just don't like her."

Oona put down her phone. "Why?"

The doorbell rang again. Wade came out from the kitchen. "You guys going to get that or what?"

Charley opened the front door.

"Hey, guys," Marisa said anxiously. "Oh, hey, Oona."

"Hi, Marisa," Oona said, blushing a little.

Geez, Charley thought. *Not you, too.*

"Your brother fill you in?"

"Uh-huh," Charley said. "I got the money." She patted her pocket as if to say, *Safe and sound.*

"Okay . . ." Marisa said, aware she was missing something but not eager to find out what.

"Oh, we're coming with you," Charley said.

"Look, I really don't think that's such a great idea," Marisa said warily.

"Nah, it's cool," Charley said. "Besides, we don't want you to have to drive all the way back to the lot by yourself."

Charley could tell Marisa wasn't buying it. She knew she was being bullied into bringing Greg's little sister and her friends along for the ride. But Charley had all the power in the situation. If Marisa tried to lay down the law and refused to take them with her, Charley could always tell her mom about the car. Or simply run up into her room with the money, lock the door, and refuse to come out.

Marisa looked Charley up and down. "Fine. But if you guys come along—"

"You're the boss, got it."

The four of them headed out, but then Charley stopped at the door.

"Wait, Oona. You better leave your phone here."

"Why?"

"In case your parents check your location again."

"Okay," Oona said. "But wait. What if they actually text me?"

"Won't they just assume that you aren't texting back because you're still mad at them?"

"Oh, right," Oona said.

"Oh my god," Wade groaned. "Did you forget you're even fighting with them?"

"Shut up, Wade." Oona went to put her phone on the end table, then hesitated. "But Charley, I need my phone. To . . . you know . . . record my thoughts."

"Maybe you can just think your thoughts," Wade said. "You know, like normal people."

Oona opened her mouth to say something really colorful.

"Never mind," Charley said, stepping between them. "You can use mine till we get back."

Oona took Charley's phone and put hers on the end table. "Okay, I guess that would work."

"Wonderful," Wade said. "Can we go now?"

They piled into Marisa's car. Wade rode shotgun. Charley and Oona were in the back, where she was giving Oona the full run-down about how she got detention from Mr. Bonino.

"It's not even a bad word," Charley huffed. "It was on a Looney Tunes cartoon, for Pete's sake."

"No way," Oona said. "Then why did he give you a detention?"

"I don't know. 'Cause he's a jerk, that's why."

Wade started to turn his head, but Charley kneed the back of his seat before he could chime in.

Ten minutes later, they pulled into the Daftari Towing and

Impound lot. Marisa had barely put her car in park before Greg bolted out of the office to meet them.

"Did you get it?" he asked anxiously.

Charley handed him the money. Marisa had texted him that she was bringing his sister and her friends, and he'd wisely known better than to make a thing about it. Still, the look on his face told Charley that once this was all settled, there would be a thing later.

They all followed Greg into the office, tripping the shop-keeper's bell above the door. A tall man in his fifties immediately came out from the back room. He had salt-and-pepper hair and wore a red soccer jersey over his dress shirt that said SIMBA SPORTS FOOTBALL CLUB across the chest with a lion underneath.

Greg counted out the bills and put them on the counter. "There it is, Mr. Daftari. Four hundred dollars in cash."

"Okay, okay. Slow down," the tall man said as he checked his watch, then rubbed his temple with his other hand. "You have the title?" he asked. There was hesitation in his voice.

"Title?" Greg asked.

Mr. Daftari turned his head to clear his throat. "I can't release the car without the title."

"You never said that!"

"I'm sorry, sir . . ."

"You never said that!!"

A young girl, presumably his daughter, came out from the back to see what the commotion was about. She looked like she was around Charley's age, wore glasses, and held a book in her hand, with a finger keeping the page. She said something in a language Charley didn't recognize, and Mr. Daftari responded in kind. The girl then looked at Charley and the others and returned to the back room.

Mr. Daftari turned back to Greg. "I really am sorry. But there's nothing more I can do right now."

Greg was too flustered and upset to form recognizable words, so Marisa took him outside to get some air. Mr. Daftari sat down and busied himself at his computer. Charley saw him check his watch again, but he caught her eye and made like he was just scratching his wrist.

"C'mon," Charley said as she led Wade and Oona outside.

Greg and Marisa were sitting on a bench outside the office. She rubbed his back while he whimpered into his hands.

"There's something up with that guy," Wade said.

Oona scoffed. "Figures you'd say that."

"Come on. First the credit card machine doesn't work. Then, the cost to get the car back is almost double the usual rate. *Then* he asks for the title?"

"That was strange," Marisa threw in. "He didn't say anything about that earlier."

"And the way he was talking with his daughter."

If Oona were a cat, you could have seen all the hairs on her back shoot straight up. "Which way was *that*, Wade?"

Aw, nuts, Charley thought. *Here it comes*. This was going to be unpleasant.

"Not in English? You mean that way, Wade?"

"Hey! I didn't say that."

"You were thinking it."

"Oh, you're a mind reader, now?"

"You know, people are still allowed to speak other languages in America. At least the last time I checked."

Charley pinched the bridge of her nose with her fingers.

"Oh, please," Wade groaned. "That's not what I meant and you know it."

"And for your information, they were speaking Swahili."

"Really? You just happen to know Swahili?"

"No, but the jersey he's wearing is for a soccer team in Tanzania. And in Tanzania, they speak Swahili. So it fits."

"But you don't know for a *fact* he's Tanzanian. Technically, you're just *inferring* it."

"It's a logical assumption."

"Got it. So when you do it, it's logic, but when I do it, I'm a—"

"Oh, real clever, Wade," Oona cut him off. "Hey, Fox News called, they want their false equivalency back!"

"Okay, both of you stop!" Charley shouted.

They did.

Charley looked over at Greg and Marisa. "When you first came in the office, was there a sign on the counter or anything that said the credit card machine was down?"

"No," Greg said.

Marisa caught on to Charley's train of thought. "Actually, he didn't mention it until after we told him which car we wanted."

"And that's when he jacked up the price?"

"Yeah," Marisa said.

Charley scratched her head. It didn't add up. If Mr. Daftari was shaking them down for more money, why would he be playing this game with the title? Wouldn't he just take them for all the cash they had and call it a night?

At the same time, Mr. Daftari was clearly lying about the credit card machine, and about needing to see the title. Charley could tell he was lying because he was bad at it, nervous and uncomfortable. He stammered and looked away when he spoke to them. Being dishonest or deceitful did not come naturally to this guy. Whatever game Mr. Daftari was playing with them, the smart money said he didn't want to be playing it. So why was he?

Then there was his daughter. Though Charley obviously couldn't know what the girl and her father had said to each other, the expression on her face when she'd glanced their way wasn't hard to translate. She was concerned, maybe even a little afraid. Something was wrong.

Charley turned to Wade. "Okay. Let's assume he is lying. Why?"

Wade shook his head. "Don't know. At first I thought he was just trying to get more money out of Greg. But now, I don't think so."

"Me neither. But then, what is going on?"

"Well," Wade started, cringing at the thought. "I think it has something to do with the car."

"Like what?'

"Like maybe something . . . happened to it?"

"What?" Greg hopped up from the bench. "Why would you even say that?!"

"Because, I don't see it," Wade said, pointing around at all the cars in the lot. "And you'd think it'd be close to the front, considering it was just brought in."

"Maybe," Charley said, trying to work it out. "Only why doesn't Mr. Daftari just say so?"

"Because it's *supposed* to be here," Wade said. "I think it might be lost."

"Aw, man," Greg wailed desperately as Marisa led him back to the bench. "I'm dead. Dead, buried, and pushing up daisies! This is the worst!"

"What if he's just stalling?" Charley suggested. "Till he can find it?"

Wade shrugged. "Maybe, yeah."

It made perfect sense. Mr. Daftari wasn't trying to get more money; he was trying to buy time. That's why he kept checking his watch.

Now the question was, what were they going to do about it?

Charley thought for a moment. She had an idea. It was a long shot, but then again, if Wade was right, it wasn't like they had anything to lose.

"Wade, you're buddies with Parker Nadal, right?"

"Yeah, so what?"

"Think he'd do us a favor?"

Wade shrugged. "I can ask. What did you have in mind?"

FOUR

9:07 P.M.

Parker Nadal. The boy of a thousand voices.

He was a seventh grader like Charley. She knew him a little, but they didn't have any classes together. He was average height with thick, unruly hair and a plump little belly he liked to drum whenever he was pondering something. Parker Nadal was also gifted with a downright uncanny ability to mimic voices.

He could do anyone. And not just famous people. Once Parker Nadal heard someone talk for long enough, they were his. He owned them, vocally speaking. And of course, that meant trouble. Parker spent a good deal of sixth grade in the principal's office for repeatedly calling the school switchboard and disguising himself as teachers, parents, even the head of the school board. So his parents, desperate to channel his gifts in a direction less detrimental to his permanent record, had built him a recording studio in the family basement.

Since then Parker spent a lot of his time redubbing many of his favorite television shows and movies—basically making anyone from SpongeBob SquarePants to Captain America to German Chancellor Angela Merkel say whatever he wanted them to—and then posting the doctored videos online under the heading "At Least That's How I Heard It."

Wade called Parker and told him what they were looking to do.

"Sure! No problem, Wade," Parker said. "You want to text me my lines?"

"Actually, is it all right if we come to you?" Wade asked. "We might need to improvise a bit."

"Yeah, okay," Parker said. "But come around the side. My dad just finished a thirty-hour rotation at the hospital. I don't want the doorbell to wake him up."

"Got it. Thanks, Parker." Wade hung up and reported back to Charley.

"You know what to have him say?" she said.

"I think so. Aren't you coming?"

Charley shook her head as they walked to Marisa's car. "Oona and I are going to stay here with Greg." She had a hunch about the girl in the back room, and she'd need to be close by if she was right. "Think you can handle riding alone with Marisa?" she teased.

"Probably better than you can." He smirked as he got into the car.

"Harsh."

"A darkness, both literal and figurative, hung over the impound lot. As the night deepened, so did the collective despair among the group. Their fellowship, for the time at least, suddenly cleaved into two halves.

"Greg, constantly teetering on the edge of a full-scale panic attack, retreated back inside the office, fearing that if he stayed outside too long, Mr. Daftari might lock him out and close up for the night.

"Charley paced in frustration while her mind worked furiously to plot the group's next move as her best friend, Oona, kept faithful counsel by her side.

"Meanwhile, Greg's exquisite and all-around inspiring girlfriend, Marisa, was bravely and selflessly driving north, along with the dim-witted mouth breather whom Charley long ago befriended out of pity like a mangy—"

"What's your deal with Wade anyway?" Charley interrupted.

Oona put the phone down. "What?"

"You heard me. You've been taking shots at him all night."

"I don't like him, Charley. He's a . . . well, let's just say we have different beliefs."

Charley gave her friend a funny look. "Beliefs?"

Oona shrugged.

"Just say it, Oona."

"Fine. Bryce Spenser."

"What about Bryce Spenser?"

"Wade called him a name."

"He called him . . . a name?"

"Don't say it like that. He called him a very offensive name. A slur."

Charley had heard something about Wade and Bryce getting into it during gym class a few weeks ago. Charley hadn't given it much thought at the time. Wade had never brought it up and, besides, Charley didn't like Bryce.

He was a theater kid, like Oona. Drama was his thing. Both performing and causing it, from what Charley could tell. He had a big personality, not to mention a big mouth, and he was good at using both to make other people feel small.

"Bryce Spenser is a jerk," Charley said.

"No, he's not. And even if he were, that doesn't mean he should be subjected to hate speech."

"What did Wade say, exactly?"

Oona didn't want to repeat it but was eventually coaxed to whisper it into Charley's ear, even though there was no one within a hundred feet of them.

"And you heard this?"

"I wasn't there," Oona admitted. "But Bryce told me all about it. He was practically in tears."

"Well, I *highly* doubt Wade would say that. If he did, then it was wrong, and I'll have plenty to say to him about it. But, he is my friend, Oona."

"Yeah, well. Maybe he shouldn't be."

"Or maybe," Charley shot back, "I just might know Wade Harris a little better than you know Bryce Spenser."

Oona flinched at that. Charley felt bad for snapping at her friend, and neither of them spoke for a while. Then Charley spied a convenience store across the street.

"Let's go get a soda or something."

"Yeah, okay," Oona said, eager to take the olive branch. "Should we see if Greg wants to come with us?"

Charley shook her head. "He won't leave the office."

Oona thought for a moment. "Why don't you guys go and I'll wait in the office."

"I don't know," Charley said.

"He needs a change of scenery," Oona insisted. "He's going stir-crazy in there."

There was no denying that. The girls went back into the office, tripping the shopkeeper's bell, which caused Mr. Daftari to look up quickly, frown, and return to his magazine. Greg was twitching and pacing around the little office like a toddler who had knocked back a bottle of apple juice and couldn't find the bathroom. It took a lot of coaxing, but the girls finally convinced him to step out for some fresh air.

Charley and Greg didn't talk as they walked away from the impound lot. Charley was still mad at him for ditching her and Wade, and Greg was annoyed that Charley had made Marisa bring her and her friends to the lot.

"Derrick's going to kill me if we don't get that car back," Greg said finally.

"We'll get it back," Charley assured him.

"You know, his uncle left him that car," Greg said. "His favorite uncle."

Charley didn't know it was a *favorite* uncle. Then again, she and Derrick never really talked that much. They had never hit it off the way Greg and Derrick did.

"If I can't get the car before he and Mom come home . . . I don't know how I'll even face him."

They crossed the street just after a white Cadillac Escalade pulled into the convenience store, hair metal blaring loudly on the car stereo. The Escalade parked diagonally across two spaces, then four guys climbed out and went inside.

They say you can't judge a book by its cover. But sometimes, you really can. Even if Charley ignored the three sleeveless pastel T-shirts, two pairs of tiger-print camo pants, and at least one puka shell necklace, she could still tell those guys were clearly, categorically obnoxious by the way they strutted through the glass double doors side by side so that anyone wanting to exit had to step back and wait.

Charley and Greg entered the convenience store a minute or two later. Right away she spotted the four jerks over by the soda dispensers, where they were harassing some poor guy in a blue hoodie. He looked like he was about Greg's age, maybe a little older. But he was smaller than Greg, with bushy hair and thick glasses, both of which looked like they were too big for his head. He was the kind of guy who attracted bullies like a magnet.

"Guys, I just want to be on my way—" Blue Hoodie pleaded as he tried to pass.

"Dude, chillax," one of the jerks said. The one wearing the puka necklace, naturally. "We're just talking."

"Yeah," one of the Camo Pants said. "Don't be rude, man."

This isn't going to end well, Charley thought to herself.

Greg noticed it, too. "Stay here," he said to Charley.

Charley knew her brother. He was going to get into the middle of it. He didn't care how badly he was outnumbered. He'd always been that way; he'd stand up to anyone if he had to. No matter how stupid an idea it was.

"Wait," Charley said. "What about we play the line game?"

Greg gave her a look.

The line game.

Greg had come up with it when Charley was eight. It was a few months after their dad had passed away, when she was still really sad but maybe ready to try, for a little bit at a time anyway, being okay again. Greg had invented the game as a way to keep Charley entertained whenever they were stuck waiting around somewhere. Like waiting for a table at a restaurant, or standing in line at the amusement park.

What you did was you started talking just a little too loudly, not enough to be super obvious, but just enough so that it was easy for people near you to eavesdrop. Then you saw how far you could go.

For instance, Charley might start by asking Greg how his shoulder was doing. He might answer with something about x-rays or physical therapy. Then Charley would ask him, how many times is this? And Greg would respond with, "Well, this is the third time I've dislocated it, if you don't count when I broke my collarbone."

Now at this point at least a couple people are listening in, which means pushing the story further. Greg might choose to be a rodeo clown trying to earn enough money to pay for college, or he might let slip that he's getting tired of being Tom Holland's stunt double.

People probably caught on that it was a gag, though no one ever said anything because that would mean admitting that they were eavesdropping. Charley never cared either way, the fun was in trying to one-up Greg. To catch him off guard, even make him laugh. She missed that.

"You think it would work?"

"Worth a shot," Charley said.

Greg looked at her and shook his head with a chuckle. Charley imagined he was remembering the receiving line at Cousin Jeremy's wedding, where Charley had half the bride's side believing she was both a chess prodigy and a compulsive pyromaniac. "All right. Why not?"

Charley nodded. "I'll go first. Come in when I scratch my neck."

Greg eased over to the coolers as Charley made her way to the soda dispensers. She pretended not to notice the four tools and focused all her attention on the guy in the blue hoodie.

"Peter? Peter Russo?" Charley said loudly.

"Um, me?" the poor guy said.

"I thought that was you," she said, slapping him on the arm. "It's me, Denise." She was close enough to him now that she could give him a heavy look that screamed, "Just go with it!"

This was the moment of truth. Greg grabbed a soda can from the cooler. He was an all-league shortstop and if things turned sour, one of those jerks was about to get a throw to first in the old melon.

"Denise," Hoodie said, nodding slowly. "Right. Good to see you."

Charley turned around toward the four jerks. "My old guitar teacher," she said with a *can-you-believe-it* crack of the voice as she scratched her neck. "Used to live down the block from me. I mean, what are the odds?"

Poor Blue Hoodie laughed nervously.

"Denise!" Greg said, wandering over. "Come on, we need to— hey, is that Peter?"

"Hi?" Blue Hoodie yelped desperately.

Greg gave him a big hug.

"How you doing, man?"

"Oh," Blue Hoodie warbled wretchedly. "Fine?"

"How's your brother Billy?" Charley said.

"Still crazy, I bet," Greg said with a laugh. "Am I right?"

"Yeah, well. You know . . . Billy."

Greg and Charley laughed. Blue Hoodie tried to join in, but it came out more like a confused whimper.

"Seriously, though," Greg said, getting things back on track. "I lost touch with him after he enlisted."

"Jackie Wilson's older sister said he's in Special Forces now," Charley volunteered helpfully. "Teaches hand-to-hand combat to Navy SEALS or something."

"Billy was always good with a knife," Greg said sagely.

Puka and his pals were really confused. And a little unnerved. Either way, Charley hoped they'd lose interest soon. The suffocating scent of their collective body sprays was making her light-headed. The game seemed to be working, though. She and Greg just needed an out, a way to get rid of these guys while making them feel like it was their idea.

"Yo," Camo Pants said to Puka. "What's going on?"

"Man, I can't believe we ran into you," Greg said. "Hey, let me get a picture for my Instagram."

There it was.

"Me too," Charley said, squeezing between her brother and Blue Hoodie.

"I can't get you in the frame," Greg said to his sister, then turned his attention to Puka. "Hey, would you mind taking our picture?"

"What?" Puka sneered. "No way. Get bent, loser. We're out of here."

Charley and Greg watched as the Escalade pulled out of the lot, and then they turned their attention back to Blue Hoodie.

"Hi. I'm Charley," she said, extending her hand. "Charley Decker. This is my brother, Greg."

"Oscar Zelzah," the guy said, taking her hand.

"You okay?" Greg said.

Oscar nodded as his knees buckled. "That was really weird. But kind of brilliant. Thank you both so much."

They waited another few minutes to be sure, and then the three of them walked back to the impound lot with their drinks. Oscar explained that he was a freshman at Northwestern University, where he was currently pledging a fraternity. Earlier tonight the older fraternity brothers had dropped him and his fellow pledges off at various random locations with no phone, wallet, or other resources. Each pledge then had to figure out, on his own, how to get back to the fraternity house. They claimed it built character.

"That's cruel," Charley scoffed.

"It's a little cruel," Oscar conceded. "But most of the time it's fairly harmless. We were all let out near El stations or bus stops. Ordinarily, everyone makes it back by midnight and then the brothers take us out for all-night pancakes. The thing is, I have a really, really lousy sense of direction. I've been at school for almost a year and I still can't find my way around campus. It's like everywhere I turn, there's the lake again."

"Come on," Greg said. "I'm sure it's not that bad. Where did they drop you off?"

"Winnetka."

"Seriously?"

"I know."

"That's like two stops *north* of campus. How did you get all the way down here?"

Oscar hung his head in shame. "What can I say? I could get lost in a swivel chair."

"Never mind, Oscar," Charley said. "You're with us now. We'll get you back to campus, one way or another."

Oona met them at Mr. Daftari's office door. "Charley, your phone," she said, handing it over. "You got a text."

"It's from Wade," Charley said, reading. "They just got to Parker's."

"Are you mad?" one very large, very burly dude said into his phone. "You're mad, aren't you?"

"Is he mad?" asked a second burly dude. "He's mad, isn't he?"

The two men sat in a booth in a pancake house off the interstate. They were brothers, identical twins actually. They both wore jeans and flannel shirts, but different flannel shirts so no one (including them) would get confused as to which brother was which.

The Woznikowski brothers. Jed and Ned. Or Ned and Jed. Truth was, even they weren't always sure.

"Uh-huh," said the one on the phone, Jed (probably). "But, geez. How is that our fault, AP? We did just like you said."

When it comes to twins, there's usually a front twin and a follow twin. The front twin is the bossier, take-charge one. A little behind, and off to the side, is the follow twin. He's usually the younger one, the quieter one, the one who looks a little less like *them*.

"What's he mad about?" Ned whispered to Jed's free ear. "We did just like he said."

The Woznikowski twins had never really figured out who was the front and who was the follow. They were two guys perpetually standing before an open doorway waiting for the other one to go inside first.

Fortunately Jed and Ned had always had AP to lead the way.

The twins gave him that nickname in high school, both because it was their friend's initials and because of all the Advanced Placement classes he took. (It was their one and only foray into wordplay, but at least they went out winners.) AP was *him* enough for all of them, which was why he'd been telling the twins what to do for about as long as they could remember.

"AP, we did," Jed protested into his phone. "You said you'd have one of your cars waiting in the parking lot . . . That was so your car. We was both there when you bought it, for Pete's sake . . . Well, who else has that same car? I thought that was the whole point . . . Yeah, AP. Okay, AP. Uh-huh. We'll take care of it, AP."

Jed sighed as he put his phone on the table.

"He was mad, wasn't he?"

Jed gave his brother a look. "He says we put the package in the wrong car and now we have to get it back."

"How are we supposed to do that? It's gone."

"He says he's gonna find it and tell us where to go."

They sat in the booth and stared at their food.

One of them said, "Should we still finish the pancakes?"

FIVE

"Well, well, well. And who do we have here?"

The voice was smooth and deep and made Marisa's knees buckle a little. However, it should have been coming out of the mouth of a roguishly handsome lounge singer in a smoky, after-hours jazz club. Not a nearsighted twelve-year-old boy in sweatpants standing in his parents' basement.

Marisa had to laugh—the incongruity between sound and sight was just too bizarre. "Marisa Ng," she said, extending her hand.

"Enchanté," the boy crooned as he kissed her hand.

"Parker," Wade said gruffly. "I need you to focus."

"Right. Sorry, Wade," Parker Nadal said in his normal voice. Or, at least, *a* normal voice. With Parker, you could never be sure. "Follow me."

He led them to a little soundproof room with a state-of-the-art sound mixing console. "Welcome to my studio."

"This is amazing," Marisa said.

"Thanks," Parker said, plopping down at the console and getting to business. "So, I'm supposed to be some rich dude calling from my private jet, right?"

"Right."

Parker drummed his belly, then hit a series of buttons on the console and fiddled with some levels. Suddenly the faint sounds of wind and turbulence filled the room. "What do you think?" he asked them.

"Yeah," Wade said, blown away. "I think this will work."

"Okay. Now this guy I'm playing?"

"Derrick Edmonds."

"What voice do you want me to use?"

"I don't know." Wade shrugged. "Any voice. Just make one up."

"I can't *make up* a voice," Parker said. "I need someone to imitate."

A confused, slightly panicked look took over Wade's face.

Marisa weighed in. "The most important thing is that it's intimidating." She thought for a moment. "Wade says you can do all the teachers at your school."

"Absolutely. Piece of cake."

"So, who's the most intimidating teacher?"

There was no need for deliberation. "Mr. Hastings," the boys both said simultaneously.

The three of them then mapped out a rough idea of what Parker was going to say when he called the impound lot. Then he tried it out using the Mr. Hastings voice.

"Wow," Marisa said. "That was good."

It really was. Mr. Hastings had been an inspired choice. He had a deep, booming voice that struck fear into anyone within earshot. He didn't even have to be mad, or actually talking to you, for that matter. Just passing Mr. Hastings's classroom and hearing the man's voice from the hall was enough to make a kid instantly slow down, check his mouth for gum, and forget the capital of Maine. When Mr. Hastings spoke, people waited for lightning, or at the very least a thunderclap or two, to end his sentences for him.

"You think?" Parker said hopefully.

"Dude, I'm shaking," Wade said.

Even Marisa was a little rattled. "That's what your teacher sounds like?"

Parker nodded. "And that's not even the mad voice."

He practiced his lines a few times as he fiddled some more with the controls on his sound system.

"Okay," Parker said finally. "I think we're ready."

He hit a few buttons on his console as the entire room now sounded like the pressurized cabin of a private jet. Satisfied, he then took a long sip from his mug of hot lemon water, drummed his belly again, and said, "Okay. Let's do this."

He made the call, hitting the speakers so they could all hear.

"Daftari Towing."

"To whom am I speaking?" Parker intoned, his Mr. Hastings impression so impressive that Wade's tongue instinctively searched his mouth for gum to swallow.

"My name is John Daftari. How can I help you, sir?"

"Mr. Daftari, my name is Derrick Edmonds, and I believe you have my car in your lot. It's a convertible 1964 World's Fair Skyway Mustang. Raven Black, if that narrows it down for you."

There was a long pause on the other end. "Yes."

"Excellent. Now, I believe my assistant is currently there at the lot attempting to reclaim possession."

"Assistant?"

"That's right. Young man named Greg Decker. Tall. Not too bright, but he means well."

Marisa gave Parker a smack on the arm.

"Ow," he said, then quickly hit the mute button. "Cut it out."

"Stop screwing around," Marisa said.

"I know what I'm doing," Parker insisted. "There's an art to this."

Wade sighed, "Parker . . ."

"Fine."

Parker turned off the mute. "My apologies, Mr. Daftari. Now, I'm going to need you to release that car."

"I can't do that, sir. Your assistant doesn't have the necessary paperwork."

"Is that so?"

"I'm afraid it is."

Parker hit a couple of buttons and then switched seamlessly into a woman's voice. "Mr. Edmonds, I'm sorry to interrupt. But the captain wanted me to tell you that we'd be landing at Midway in about twenty minutes."

"Thank you, Sheila," Parker said, back in his Mr. Hastings voice, which, Wade noticed, was starting to take on a bit of a Texas twang. "Alrighty now. Here's where we're at, Mr. Daftari. One of two things is going to happen. Either my assistant is going to pay to get my car out of your lot so he can come pick me up at the tarmac, or I'm going to have to call my lawyer and have him come get me. And then the two of us can just come to you and we'll straighten this all out together. Sound like a plan to you, Mr. Daftari?"

There was a long pause on the other end. "Let me see what I can do and get back to you, Mr. Edmonds."

"That would be splendid. I look forward to hearing from you."

Parker ended the call.

"I think that went rather well," he said.

"What do we do now?" Marisa asked.

"Well, now I text Charley and Oona and we see what happens on their end."

"Oona Adair?" Parker perked up. "The theater girl that's always talking into her phone?"

"Yeah. What about her?"

"Why does she do that anyway?"

"She thinks her life is a novel and she's the narrator."

Parker considered. "Dude. That's wild."

Wade looked up from his phone. "Okay, sent."

"Good," said Marisa. "We should probably get back to the impound lot."

"Take me with you," Parker said.

"No way," Marisa balked.

"Come on. I want to see how this all plays out," he begged.

Wade pulled Marisa aside. "Actually, I think we should bring him with us."

"What? Why?"

"Well, the thing with Parker is that, when it comes to prank calls, he kind of doesn't know when to stop."

"Oh, peachy."

"Yeah, that's how he always gets caught. The first call goes off without a hitch. But then he has to keep calling back to see how far he can press his luck."

"So, you're saying that if we don't take him with us, then once we leave he might call Mr. Daftari back . . ."

"And blow the whole thing. Yeah."

"Wonderful."

Wade turned back to Parker. "Okay, you're in."

"Sweet!"

Marisa gave Wade a skeptical look.

"Hey, you never know. We might need him again."

"The call had been made. There was nothing to do now but wait. Greg was inside the office with Oscar, the college student they'd rescued from the convenience store aggro-bros.

"Oona and Charley hovered closer to the building, watching, listening, waiting. Silence was their watchword."

Charley gave her an annoyed look.

"Silence was their watchword."

Charley gave her a more annoyed look.

"Sorry," Oona whispered and stepped away to continue her narration.

Charley made her way toward the back of the building, where she didn't even need to press her ear to the wall to hear Mr. Daftari ranting desperately in agitated frustration. As near as she could make out, he was in that back room. Charley then heard his daughter respond in a calm, reassuring cadence.

A few minutes later, Mr. Daftari returned to the front office. Charley watched from the window as the man called her brother to the counter. She could hear Mr. Daftari telling Greg that he was trying to work something out, and to please be patient.

He's playing for time, Charley thought.

Then she heard a door open in the back of the building. She crept closer as she watched Mr. Daftari's daughter wander out into the lot while she dialed on her phone. Charley followed.

"Amir," the girl barked into the mouthpiece. "You need to come back *now*. This is serious."

She hung up the phone and then looked around suspiciously. Charley crouched behind the corner of the building and held her breath.

It didn't help. The girl walked straight toward her.

"My name is Michaela," she said, looking Charley straight in the eye. "We should probably talk."

"My brother has your car," Michaela said to Charley a few moments later when Oona had joined them. "He didn't steal it or anything. He just wanted to show it to his friends."

"I totally get it," Charley said. "We don't care about that, really. We're not looking to get anyone in trouble. We just need the car back. Can you help us?"

"I've been trying to call him, but he won't answer." Then she said, "I can track him, though."

"No way. How?"

"I did a jailbreak on his phone for him."

"Wow," Oona said, impressed. "Cool."

She shrugged. "It wasn't hard." Michaela, it turned out, went to a STEM school and was really good with electronics. "He wanted these inappropriate emojis for texting and I agreed, mostly on principle. Free speech and whatnot. You know, every-one's so convinced that a robotic uprising is going to be all SkyNet and Terminators. Or Cylons, if BSG is more your jam. But the cold, hard truth is that the robots don't need to take us over.

They're already in control. We're all slaves to our cell phones, especially the social media apps. And don't even get me started on that new Ursula—"

Oona let out a little squeak that loosely translated to *You complete me.*

"Sorry." Michaela shrugged a bit sheepishly. "I tend to go on a bit."

Charley had to laugh. "No. You really don't."

"Anyway, the point is, when I did the jailbreak, I also hacked into the locator app on my brother's phone. I don't like to use it, but I can find out where he is without him knowing."

"That's so cool!" Oona exclaimed with a laugh that made Charley feel increasingly like a conversational third wheel.

Michaela blushed a little. "Thanks. The thing is, I don't want my dad to know where Amir is until we get the car back."

"I don't follow you," Oona said.

Charley did. "You want to get the car back without ratting out your brother."

Michaela nodded.

"Okay, deal."

Michaela opened the tracking app on her phone.

"I'm such an idiot," Michaela said. "It's Friday. Of course. That should have been the first place I looked."

"How far away is he?"

"A few blocks. We can totally walk it."

"Okay," Charley said. "Give me a minute."

Charley poked her head in the office. Greg sat with Oscar, talking quietly.

"So, once you get your car out of impound, you can give me a ride back to campus?"

"Sure," Greg said. "But right now it's *if* I can get the car out of impound."

"Hey," she said, giving Greg a *come outside* jerk of the head.

Greg followed her out. "What's up?"

"I think I can get the Mustang back."

"That's great! Let's go!"

"But I need you to stay here."

"Why?"

"We need things to seem normal. Well, normal for this situation." Charley reasoned that as long as Greg was in the waiting area, Mr. Daftari would stay behind the counter to keep an eye on him, to see if he was talking on the phone with anyone about the car, like Derrick, or worse, Derrick's lawyers. But if Greg left, Mr. Daftari might go looking for his daughter, who wouldn't be there because she was with Charley and Oona getting the Mustang back.

"Okay," Greg said uncertainly. "I think I got about half of that."

"Look, the bottom line is that if you want the car back, you're going to have to trust me."

Greg made a pained *I'm-not-so-sure* face.

"Or we can just go home and explain it all to Derrick tomorrow."

"No!" Greg exclaimed, panic dancing in his eyes. "We can't do that, Charley! We just can't!"

Charley couldn't believe this was the same big brother who half an hour ago was ready to take on four guys in a convenience store. It was so weird; Greg never got like this. He *never* stressed this much. Not even about getting in trouble. When things went sideways, he just shrugged and took his lumps.

But he sure was stressing out now. He was so emotional he could hardly think straight anymore. And all this talk about *Derrick's gonna kill me! I can't even face him!*—she had no idea where that was coming from. Charley wasn't Derrick's biggest fan, but the guy had zero temper. He was one of those *I'm-not-mad-I'm-just-disappointed* adults.

Maybe that was it, though. Maybe what Greg was really so frightened of was letting Derrick down. Charley didn't get it, but there it was. Greg really liked Derrick. And Marisa. And, apparently, Canada.

"Let me do this, Greg," Charley insisted. "It'll be okay. I promise."

Michaela led Charley and Oona out the back gate, through an alley, and down a residential street.

"He's still there," Michaela said, tracking her brother on her phone. "We should have your car back in no time."

"Can I ask you something?" Charley said.

"Sure."

"It's just, for someone against tech overreach, you don't seem to have much problem using it to spy on your older brother. Not that I'm judging," Charley added quickly.

"That's a fair point," Michaela conceded. "But you know what they say: You can't put the genie back in the bottle. Best you can do is be smart with your wishes. Besides, it's kind of hard to stand on principle when your dad's garage is about to get sued into oblivion."

Charley cringed and rubbed the back of her neck. "Yeah, Michaela. About that . . ." She took a deep breath, then came clean about pranking Michaela's dad. It probably wasn't the smart play, but it felt like the right one. Michaela was really cool, and they did share the sacred bond of idiot older brothers.

Michaela stopped for a moment, her face inscrutable. Charley worried that she had seriously miscalculated the situation.

But then Michaela just laughed and started walking again. "Okay," she said with a nod of respect. "Good to know."

After a couple of blocks they turned a corner and came upon an intersection. At the far corner was a car wash. The car wash was closed, naturally, but along the perimeter of the parking lot were several pop-up food stands, each one featuring a different kind of culinary street fare. It was kind of like a farmers market, but at night. And a lot cooler.

"This is amazing!" Oona exclaimed as they entered the parking lot.

Michaela stopped suddenly.

"Follow my lead," she said to Charley.

Charley nodded, then Michaela started yelling angrily in Swahili as she marched ahead of the girls toward the center of the parking lot, where three young men were hanging out around...

The Mustang.

"You idiot!" Michaela said, now in English, to the one Charley pegged as her brother. "Do you have any idea the trouble you've caused, Amir?"

"Michaela, relax," Amir said smoothly.

"Oh, I'd love to. Only the owner of that car is on his way to the lot right now. With his lawyers!"

Amir gulped. "Lawyers?"

"Uh-huh. He called them from his *private jet* after he chewed Dad out and threatened to sue. Which you would have known if you had bothered to answer my calls."

Amir's knees turned to jelly. "Private jet?"

"Yep."

"Michaela," Amir said, taking his sister by the arm. "What do we do?"

Michaela snuck a little smile Charley's way before answering her brother. "Well, if we don't want Dad to lose his business, you're going to get the car back and apologize profusely."

"Done. Of course."

"Good. But first you're going to buy us all food." She turned to Charley and Oona. "You guys hungry? Because the truck over there does the best empanadas."

"You ever going to tell your brother the truth?" Charley asked between mouthfuls of ground beef.

The girls were at the lot, sitting on the ground with their backs up against the office wall. They'd gotten the food to go, of course. Greg was inside talking with Mr. Daftari, who Charley had to say was taking it all really well. He'd been so glad to see the Mustang back in the lot in one piece that he hadn't gotten mad at all with Michaela for sneaking off to get it back without telling him. He wasn't even that mad at Amir, who'd returned the car with such effusive apologies and tearful promises of repentance that any displays of temper would have seemed redundant anyway.

Michaela shook her head as she swallowed her food. "No way. Amir pulls this sort of stuff all the time. He's got this coming. Besides, he ruined my Friday Movie Night."

"What's Friday Movie Night?" Oona asked.

"Every Friday, I spend the night at the lot with my dad. I don't get to see him that much during the week, so this is kind of our one big chance to hang out, just the two of us. We order takeout and watch movies. He makes the couch up into a bed for me. It sounds kind of silly, I know."

"No, it doesn't," Charley said.

"Don't get me wrong. Tonight was kind of fun. Eventually, I mean."

83

"We could always do it again," Oona threw in. "Not the bit with the car, of course. But we could always hang out again. All three of us."

"Really?"

"Absolutely," Charley agreed.

Michaela thought for a moment. "I'd like that," she said.

Around this time Marisa arrived back at the lot with Wade and Parker Nadal.

"Another one?" Greg groaned when he saw Parker. Marisa gave him a look that said if he still wanted to have a girlfriend tomorrow, he'd best let it go.

"Don't suppose you saved any for us?" Wade said as he and Parker walked over to the girls.

"There's a steak burrito in there," Charley said, handing him a paper take-out bag.

"Sweet."

As Wade and Parker split the burrito, Charley filled them in on everything they'd missed, and then Michaela asked Parker to re-create the prank phone call for her.

"Wow," Michaela laughed. "You guys weren't kidding. He really is the kid with a thousand voices."

"A thousand and one, now," Parker said, doing a spot-on Michaela.

"Okay, that's just scary."

In the end, Mr. Daftari didn't charge them anything for the tow. He seemed happy just to get the Mustang off his property as soon as humanly possible.

As they said their goodbyes, Charley and Michaela put their contact info in each other's phones.

"I put Oona's in there, too," Charley said as she handed Michaela's back.

"Perfect," Michaela said. Then: "Is she really running away from home?"

Charley gave an iffy kind of flutter of the hand. "It's kind of a family ritual. Her version of Friday Movie Night."

"And so, the Fellowship of the Lost Mustang was reunited. Greg and Marisa loaded up their cars, and they all drove back to the campus of Northwestern University, where the intrepid young Oscar, safe from the tacky convenience store aggro-bros, was returned without further ado to his college brethren. The elders of his fraternity, he learned, had been deeply worried about their wayward comrade ..."

"Dude," one of the older fraternity brothers said, handing Oscar back his cell phone. "You need to call your mom. Pronto."

Oscar looked at his phone. There were six voice mail messages and about thirty texts from his mom, the last one warning that if she didn't hear from him soon, she was going to contact the state police.

"Oh boy." Oscar grabbed the phone and quickly called her.

"State police?" Oona said.

"He didn't tell you?" the other fraternity brother said.

"Tell us what?"

"No, Ma. I'm fine," Oscar protested into his phone while he shooed the fraternity brothers away. "I just left my phone in my room. No, really. Everything's . . . Ma, please don't call the governor of Illinois."

Charley and Greg shared a look as Oscar talked down his mom.

"She's very protective," Oscar said after he hung up. Then: "I owe you two big-time."

"Glad we could help," Greg said.

"You'd have done the same for us," Charley joked, doing a dramatic hair flip. "Though probably with less flair."

"No doubt," Oscar laughed. "On both counts. But seriously. Either of you guys ever need anything, you call me."

Oscar walked the group to the door. "Thanks again, man," he said, shaking Greg's hand one more time. "And good luck at UBC."

"Hey, thanks."

"Man, Canada. My mom barely let me out of Indiana."

Greg gave Oscar one last wave, then the group left the fraternity and walked back to their cars.

"Well," Greg said with a heavy, peaceful cleansing breath. "I don't know about the rest of you, but I am exhausted. I can't wait to just crawl into bed and straight-up pass out."

"Here, here," said Marisa.

"Wait, what?" Charley said, her eyes narrowing. "Aren't you going to watch movies with us when we get home?"

"Charley, seriously?"

"Yeah, Greg. Seriously."

"Come on, it's late. Just give it a break."

"Greg," Marisa said in a gently warning tone.

"What? I'm tired. Aren't you tired?"

"Excuse me. You're tired?" Charley could feel the anger welling up inside her. Though a part of her knew she was overreacting, a bigger part of her didn't care. Maybe it was the stress of the last few hours catching up with her. Or Oscar mentioning Canada. For the last hour or so, she'd practically forgotten that her brother was going to the farthest-away college he could find. Though maybe, in the end, it was simply that she'd had fun tonight, and thought Greg had, too. But all her brother could think about was how tired he was. Tired of her.

The BFC was out now and in full effect. Wade and Oona reflexively took a step backward, pulling Parker with them.

"What's going on?" he whispered.

"Just don't make any sudden movements."

"You're tired?" Charley repeated. "I can't imagine why you'd be tired, Greg. All you've done tonight is lose a car. Which we found for you, if I'm not mistaken. You're welcome for that, by the way."

"Geez, Charley—"

"You know, it doesn't matter. Take us back to the house and then you can do whatever you want. Go to bed, go to Canada, lose the stupid car again for all I care. I'm done." She smacked the trunk hard with the palm of her hand.

There was an awkward silence.

"Uuuhhhnnn" came a groan from the trunk.

Followed by a considerably more awkward silence.

Charley slapped the trunk again, a little lighter.

Another, shorter groan emitted from the trunk. "Uuhhnn."

Oona said, "Okay, that sounded like . . ."

"Someone's in there," Wade said.

Parker edged away from the car. "Is there something you guys neglected to tell me?"

"Greg," Marisa said in a terrified whisper. "Unlock the trunk."

Greg did as he was told. He lifted the lid and then jumped to the side while the others tried to peek inside and stay clear at the same time.

Except for Charley, who just stood there and leaned in closer for a better look.

"Hey," she said. "I know that guy."

SIX

11:00 P.M.

"Feeling any better?"

The guy from the trunk gave Greg a slight, unconvincing nod. His shaking hands cradled a cup of coffee. His name was Mitch Rosenfeld, and he was having a really bad night.

"You aren't going to scream and run away again, are you?" Wade asked.

After Greg had opened the trunk of the Mustang, there had been a lot of screaming and running away, which was understandable. It took Greg a block and a half to catch Mitch and talk him down. Mitch managed to calm himself enough to tell them his name. But then, when they asked how he had gotten into the trunk of their car, he'd started screaming all over again.

Now everyone sat on the outdoor patio of a coffee shop just

south of campus. Charley caught Mitch looking at her with sudden recognition. "You were the girl at New Farouk's," he said. "The one I ran into on the way out."

Charley nodded, remembering. "Two guys followed you outside. Were they the ones who put you in our trunk?"

"I honestly have no idea," Mitch said. "I remember going into Farouk's and sitting down at the counter. Then I felt this pinch on the back of my neck, like I got stung by a bee or something. I sort of remember leaving, but then I must have blacked out, because the next thing I know I woke up in your trunk."

"Where did you feel the sting?" Marisa asked, checking out the back of his neck.

"About there," Mitch said, pointing.

"There's a mark."

"No way! You were drugged!"

"Parker . . ."

"That is so wild!"

"Knock it off," Greg scolded. "This is serious."

"He's lucky to be alive," Oona chimed in. "If there had been the tiniest bit of air in that needle, he could have gotten an embolism and died instantaneously."

Mitch put his coffee down and swayed uneasily in his seat.

"Nah, whoever did this probably knew what they were

doing," Parker reasoned. "They'd at least want to keep him alive long enough to harvest his kidneys."

"Guys," Marisa said. "Not helping."

"Besides," Wade said. "If they wanted his organs, why did they put him in our trunk?"

"How should I know?"

"Maybe they didn't want his organs," Oona pondered. "Maybe they wanted to hunt him for sport on a remote island."

"Again, trunk."

"Guys!" Marisa scolded.

While the others argued among themselves, Charley focused on Mitch. "The two guys who followed you out," Charley said. "Did you see them?"

Mitch shook his head. "No. What did they look like?"

"Kind of big. Older but not old. I think they might have been brothers. They kind of looked the same."

Mitch put his hands on the table to steady himself. "Flannel shirts, jeans?"

"Uh-huh."

Everyone got quiet. For a second Charley thought Mitch was going to bolt again, but he didn't. "They wanted something," he said. "But it wasn't my kidneys."

Charley's first and lasting impression of Mitch Rosenfeld was that he was the kind of guy who blended into the woodwork.

He was twenty-three, just a year out of college, and worked in the accounting department at Pangea headquarters. He spent most of his days by himself, filing. The file rooms at Pangea headquarters took up the entire floor directly below Alton Peck's penthouse offices, but Mitch almost never saw the CEO. His days were peaceful, quiet, even a little dull.

Charley guessed that was how Mitch liked it. Some people want to leave their mark, to set the world on fire. Mitch Rosenfeld seemed content just to keep warm.

Then, a few days ago, Peck gave everyone at Pangea their very own Ursula, free of charge. The coolest, most coveted piece of tech in the world, and Mitch had one.

And it was completely ruining his life.

"I brought my Ursula to work with me," he explained. "To play music while I worked. And, you know, kind of keep me company."

"Sure," Greg said.

"Well, after a couple of hours I discovered a glitch. It turns

93

out that when two Ursulas are within twenty feet of each other, they automatically sync up and share all their data."

"Seriously? That's wild," Parker snickered.

"Wait," Wade said. "I thought you were all alone in the file room."

"I was."

Charley got there first. "Twenty feet goes up and down, too."

Mitch pointed at Charley. "Bingo."

"Wait," Marisa said. "You're saying that your Ursula synced with another Ursula directly above you?"

"Not just any other Ursula. Alton Peck's Ursula."

"So now everything that was on his Ursula—"

"Is now on my Ursula, too."

"And by everything, I don't suppose you mean, like, his grandmother's tuna casserole recipe?"

"I mean every single corrupt, shady, and, most importantly, criminal thing that my boss has ever done to make Pangea the most powerful company in the world. Bribery, extortion, blackmail, embezzlement, coercion, fraud, even some light treason. It's a lot."

There was a protracted silence at this point in the conversation, until Parker broke it with, "WHOOOAAA! Dude, now *that* is—"

"Wild?" Greg snapped. "Yes, Parker. It is wild. I think we all get that."

"Who were the guys at New Farouk's?" Charley cut in, getting them all back on track.

"The Woznikowski brothers," Mitch said. "Two of Alton Peck's favorite goons. I don't know exactly what they do for him, but everyone at Pangea knows to keep clear of those guys."

"And they're the ones who tried to kidnap you tonight?"

"If that's who you saw follow me out of New Farouk's, then yeah."

"Why didn't they just kill you?"

"Wade!"

"It's a valid question," Wade protested. "Obviously, it's good they didn't."

"They need him alive," Parker said sagely. "So they can torture him to find out how much he knows."

"Right. Not to mention where his Ursula is," Wade chimed in.

"Totally."

"Will you two knock it off!"

"Guys," Marisa said, calling for order. "We're getting ahead of ourselves. We still have no idea why they put poor Mitch in the trunk of *our* Mustang."

Oona, whose head had been buried in Charley's phone for the

bulk of the conversation, suddenly looked up at the others. "I think I can answer that."

"Is it the Illuminati?" Parker guessed. "It's the Illuminati."

"Go ahead, Oona," Charley said.

"Back in the fall, I read this profile on Alton Peck," Oona said, scrolling through the article on Charley's phone. "Total puff piece. I mean, they didn't even ask him about the working conditions at his Pangea fulfillment centers. You know Pangea has an app that monitors how long an employee spends in the bathroom?"

"Oona," Charley sighed.

"I know, I know. Typical *New York Times* puff piece. Why am I surprised?"

"Oona!"

"Okay, here it is," Oona said, finding the pertinent passage. "'Alton Peck's plane landed at the private airstrip he built outside his hometown of Fox Lake, Illinois. Waiting for him on the tarmac was his prized possession, a convertible Raven Black 1964 World's Fair Skyway Mustang.'"

"Let me see that," Greg said, taking the phone from Oona.

"Maybe the article got it wrong." Wade shrugged.

"Nope," Greg said, scanning the article: "Listen to this, it's a direct quote: 'My father was a car nut. He used to drag me to auto shows all the time. And the Skyway Mustang was his all-time favorite. After I made my first million, I bought one of the last remaining models to honor my father and his memory.'"

Charley said, "They thought they were putting Mitch in the back of Alton Peck's Mustang."

"Of course! Then sometime later, Alton Peck picks up the car, drives poor Mitch back to his rich guy lair, and tortures him into giving up his Ursula."

"Parker," Wade admonished.

"Sorry." Parker rolled his eyes. "*Interrogates* him into giving up his Ursula. That better?"

Mitch moaned helplessly.

"Okay," Marisa suggested. "I'm thinking this is the point in the conversation where someone suggests going to the police."

"No cops!" Mitch yelped desperately.

"Priors, huh?" Parker guessed. "Two strikes already, one more and you do state time? Am I right?"

"What is wrong with you?" Mitch wailed.

"Ignore him," Charley said, shooting Parker a look. "Why no cops?"

"Remember that earlier bit about all the bribery and extortion and coercion and blackmail? Well, he had help."

"You're saying he has cops on his payroll?"

"I'm saying he has *everyone* on his payroll. Cops, aldermen, the city comptroller, two state senators—"

"Okay," Greg cut in. "We get the picture."

"Yeah," Parker said. "You're in deep trouble."

"More like *we're* in deep trouble," Charley corrected.

"Come again?"

"She's right," Wade said. "Ten minutes after they dump this poor guy's body in Lake Michigan, those flannel goons you were talking about—"

"The Woznikowski brothers."

"—are going to be looking for the driver of the wrong Mustang."

"And everyone else who was with him."

There was a long pause while they all took a moment to consider the fragile state of their own mortality. Then Marisa said: "Where is it?"

Mitch looked confused. "Where is what?"

"The Ursula," Charley said, catching on.

"Oh, right," Mitch said. "I stashed it in a locker on my way to work this morning."

"A locker? Where?"

"Uh-huh. At Fun Never Stops. You know, the twenty-four-hour video arcade down by Grant Park?"

"Yeah," Wade said warily. "We know it. But why did you hide your Ursula there?"

"I like old video games."

"They have batting cages, too," Parker chimed in helpfully. "And go-carts."

"The go-carts aren't twenty-four hours, though," Mitch clarified. "They usually close the track around one or two."

"Good to know."

"And they also have the old-timey lockers, with an actual key. See?" Mitch said, digging into his front pocket. A look of panic came over his face. "It's gone," he said quietly.

The entire table gasped as one. Then Mitch said, "Oh, wait. Never mind. Wrong pocket. Here we go."

Mitch put the key on the table. They all stared at the little piece of metal with awe and trepidation, like looking at a rare diamond that was part hand grenade.

"I think we can all agree the first order of business is retrieving Mitch's Ursula," Greg said, picking up the key. "Then we can figure out who to give it to so that Alton Peck goes to jail for a long, long time."

"That won't be easy," Mitch said. "I'm telling you, the guy has a long, long reach."

"Greg's right," Marisa said. "But there has to be somebody

Alton Peck hasn't bought off. Somebody who will do the right thing. I'm in."

"Me too," Charley said.

Wade and Oona chimed in as well.

Parker said, "So does that mean we'll have to take two cars?"

"No," Greg said. "Because we're not all going. Charley, you and your friends walk back to our house while Marisa and I take Mitch to Fun Never Stops to get his Ursula."

"No," Charley protested. "I'm coming with you."

"Not a chance. You had your fun back at the impound lot, but this is too dangerous. I don't even want you guys going back to the car, in case those two guys are already looking for it. You're going home, Charley. Now."

"But they did not go home. Though Charley had allowed her brother to believe he'd won their battle of wills, she had no intention of going gently into her good night. Not when there were wrongs to be righted, secrets exposed, crimes avenged . . ."

"You know, you've got a real flair for that," Parker said.

Oona put down the phone and squirmed a little in her seat. "Thanks," she said, embarrassed and flattered at the same time.

Charley and Wade were sitting together on the other side of the train car. After Greg had ordered them back to the house, Charley got up from the table and just started walking away while Wade and the others followed awkwardly. Even though they were heading in the right direction, Wade knew there was no way they were actually going back to the house. Sure enough, when they hit Foster Street, instead of going straight, Charley suddenly took a hard left.

"Wait," Oona said. "Isn't this the wrong way?"

"Not for the train," Charley said.

"The train?" Wade stopped. "You want to take the El into the city? Now?"

"Why not? It might actually be safer. If those Wozni-what guys—"

"Woznikowski," Parker added helpfully.

"If those guys tracked our Mustang, then it's only a matter of time until they show up at the house."

"Uh-huh," Wade said. "Sure."

"And you did offer to take me to your uncle's club tonight."

"We're going to a club?" Oona asked, dubiously.

"Cabaret. You'll love it," Charley assured her.

Wade laughed. "All right, Decker. You want to go, let's go."

That was a little over half an hour ago.

They'd just passed Wrigley Field when Wade said, "We'll need to switch to the Brown Line at Fullerton."

"Okay," Charley said. It was the first they'd talked since Wade had laughed, a bit too ruefully in Charley's opinion, and agreed to take her to his uncle's club. "Are you mad at me?"

"No, I'm not mad," Wade said. "Greg's gonna be, though."

Charley looked away and shifted in her seat.

"But that's the plan, isn't it? Sooner or later he's going to call to check in on you. To make sure we're all back at the house like he said. Then you're going to tell him we're not."

"Why would I do that?"

"So he'll have to come get us. Because one way or another, Charley Decker is getting her milkshake tonight."

"Milkshake?" Charley looked confused for a beat. "Oh, I get it. The milkshake is a *metaphor*. You think I'm doing this to punish my brother for flaking on me."

"Aren't you?"

"Maybe. Or maybe I'm just taking your advice. You know, trying to be flexible, make the best of the situation. Because there's no reason we still can't make this an *awesome* night. Right?"

Wade didn't say anything. Sometimes that bothered Charley more than when he did.

The Woznikowski brothers drove a beat-up, maroon 1983 Chevrolet Monte Carlo with large patches of yellow Bondo putty slathered around the front and back fenders. It was a very sketchy-looking car. The kind of car you'd see in one of those educational videos about stranger danger. The kind of car just begging to be pulled over by police. It was three-and-a-half tons of probable cause.

Which is why AP had wanted them to dump the accountant in the Pangea delivery van while they broke into his apartment to look for that other Ursula.

Only AP hadn't said *delivery van*, he'd said *car*.

"There'll be a car waiting in the restaurant parking lot. Put the accountant in the back and I'll get it later, after you leave." AP was smart, but the brothers couldn't figure how anyone could say *car* when they meant *van*. And if that wasn't AP's car, his Mustang, at New Farouk's, then whose could it be?

The brothers were on their way to Evanston to find out. But then AP called Jed's cell.

"Hey there, AP," Ned said, answering his brother's phone. "Ned, here," he said, though not with complete certainty. "'Cause Jed's driving. Distracted driving isn't safe, you know."

Ned listened carefully. AP talked fast, and a lot of what he said had to do with how the twins were morons and he was running out of patience. But in between all that he also said important stuff, like what they should do next. It could be easy to miss.

"We just got off the highway," Ned said.

"Dempster," Jed added helpfully. "Tell him we're on Dempster."

"Uh-huh," Ned said into the phone. "Uh-huh." Then, to Jed: "He don't care. He said we need to turn around and go south, back toward the city."

"Aw, jeez," Jed griped as he did a U-turn across three lanes of traffic. "I wish he'd make up his darned mind."

AP was still barking into the phone at Ned, telling them to hurry and stop screwing up and things like that. The whole thing was making Ned kind of scared. AP was really mad. That wasn't it, though. AP got mad a lot, that's just how he was.

And it wasn't the kidnapping, either. They broke the law for AP all the time. Grabbing that nerdy accountant guy and throwing him in the trunk of a Mustang (the wrong Mustang, as it turned out, though he really didn't think that was their fault), that was just business as usual.

It was how AP kept telling them where to go to find the

accountant, that's what was bothering Ned. The way he knew exactly where this guy was going—there was something not right about that. It was creepy. Laws were made to be broken; Ned was good with that. But there had to be limits. You had to have *rules*.

"Where to now?" Jed grumbled when they were back on the southbound I-94 toward Chicago.

Ned put down his brother's cell phone. "He said he'd text when he had the location."

The two brothers drove in silence toward the city. Ned wondered whether Jed ever thought about this stuff. He'd never wondered what his brother thought before, about anything. It was a new feeling.

Ned didn't like it.

SEVEN

SATURDAY 12:17 A.M.

"Here?" Oona said, stopping in her tracks. "This is your uncle's club?"

"Cabaret," Wade corrected. "What's the big deal?"

"Your uncle owns *Sassy's*?"

"Co-owns, actually," Wade clarified. "With his husband."

"H-h-his husband?" Oona stammered, still struggling to process. Not that she had any trouble grasping the idea of two men marrying each other. It was just the fact one of them might be related to Wade Harris that was throwing her for a loop. But not nearly as big a loop as the revelation that Wade's uncle co-owned *the* Sassy's.

Sassy's was the most popular nightclub (correction, *cabaret*) in Chicago. But it was more than that. It was a cultural institution. In addition to a Michelin star for its food and the hottest live entertainment, Sassy's was most famous for having one of the best drag revues in the country. There was always a line out the door, even this late at night.

Not that Wade seemed to notice. He just walked right up to the front of the line, where a glowering bouncer with more muscles than an *Avengers* movie stood sentry.

What happened next nearly knocked Oona off her feet.

"Oh. Hey, Wade," the bouncer said, suddenly all smiles.

"Hi, Mickey," Wade said. "Busy night?"

"Eh, average. They all with you?"

"Yeah."

The bouncer, Mickey, looked away for a moment as he said something into his Bluetooth earpiece. "Stage door?" he said to Wade.

Wade nodded and led the group to the alley on the side of the building, where a nondescript door was opened from the inside by a statuesque drag queen in a teal sequined dress. "Wade, honey!" she squealed, wrapping him in a bear hug.

"Hey, Eve," Wade laughed.

"Sweetheart, it's been too long," Eve said. "Now get in here and bring those friends of yours."

As the others made their way inside, Oona just stood there in the alley, gobsmacked.

"You coming?" Charley said.

"What? Oh, yeah. Sorry."

Wade introduced the group as Eve led them through the backstage hallway to the dressing rooms.

"Enchanté, my lady," Parker crooned, taking Eve's hand and kissing it.

"Um, Parker," Charley said, bemused. "You do know—"

"Beauty is beauty, and must be recognized."

Eve laughed. "Does he always sound—"

Wade said, "Don't encourage him."

Backstage was a zoo, with performers bustling about in various states of dress. Some were in full costume, some were in their street clothes, a lot were in between. But they all stopped whatever they were doing to fuss and fawn over Wade like nobody's business.

"Girls, girls," Eve chided the group. "Ease up. Can't you see you're embarrassing him?" Then, to Wade: "You guys hungry? I'm sure Marco would whip something up for you."

"I could eat," Parker said instantly.

"What?" Oona scoffed. "You just had a burrito at the impound lot."

"Half a burrito," Parker corrected. "And that was, like, two hours ago."

Twenty minutes later Parker was chowing down on the best French dip sandwich he'd ever had in his life. Wade, meanwhile, had been dragged away by a flapper and a French aristocrat who needed some last-minute alterations to their costumes.

"Hands of a surgeon," Eve explained. "A couple of years ago, that kid re-stitched the entire seam on a mermaid costume in three minutes flat."

"Want some?" Parker said to Oona, waving half a sandwich at her as Eve wandered toward the dressing rooms.

"Huh? Oh. No, thanks." Oona looked around. "Where did Charley go?"

Parker responded with an indefinite grunt. Then, after swallowing: "So, what's with you?"

"Me? Nothing."

"Come on. You've been acting weird ever since we got here." Parker made a motion to indicate the room in general. "Are you uncomfortable with . . ."

"What? No! Absolutely not!"

"Okay, okay," he backed off. "Sorry."

"I just," Oona hesitated. She didn't want to say it. "Seeing Wade here, like this. It doesn't make sense."

"What do you mean?"

"Well, you know." The look on Parker's face indicated that he clearly did not. "That whole thing with Bryce Spenser. What Wade called him? In gym class?"

"Yeah. What about it?"

"I mean, he calls Bryce something like that. And then he comes here and everyone just loves him—"

"Wait a minute," Parker said, cutting her off. "Just what do you think Wade said to Bryce Spenser?"

"I'd really rather not repeat it."

"Can you give me a hint? How many syllables was it?"

"Oh, fine," Oona growled, then leaned over and whispered the word in Parker's ear.

He laughed.

"It's not funny. It's a really offensive word. To men and women, I might add."

"I know, I know," Parker placated. "But that's not what Wade called Bryce Spenser."

"It's not?"

Parker shook his head. Then he leaned over and whispered in

Oona's ear. Not that the word he whispered really needed to be whispered, but it made for nice symmetry.

"Oh," Oona gasped a little. "That's vulgar. But not offensive, identity-wise."

"And let me tell you, Bryce had it coming. I know because I was there. We were all in the locker room changing after gym class, right? And Bryce starts in on Jason Downey, making fun of his clothes because he's the youngest of four brothers and all he ever wears are hand-me-downs. Starts calling him 'Hand Me Downey,' which is a pretty good play on words, but also pretty cruel, especially coming from a rich kid like Bryce Spenser."

"And that's when Wade called Bryce . . ."

"Yep."

"Then why did Bryce tell everyone . . ."

Parker shrugged and went back to his sandwich.

Wade was busy for the next half an hour. After he made the alterations for Zelda and Patrice, Marisol had trouble with her fake lashes and Jasmine's wig was "an absolute disaster." Everyone, it seemed, needed his help. Mostly it was for old time's sake, though. Wade hadn't been around in a while and everyone missed him.

For the last couple of years, Wade had been something between a mascot and a boy Friday around the club. He had always been good with his hands, nimble and precise, so it didn't take much to get the knack for working on costumes, makeup, and hair. Every now and then some of the girls would try to rope him into one of the acts, but Wade was a strictly backstage kind of guy.

Just when Wade was starting to wonder when he'd see his uncle Terry, Mickey poked his head in the dressing room. "Boss says to come up when you're done here."

A few minutes later, Wade went upstairs to his uncle's office. The room always looked more like a den or a study than a place dedicated to running the hippest cabaret in the city. But then Uncle Terry resembled a retired schoolteacher more than a club owner. Very tall and thin, with a mop of wavy gray hair and a slight, distinguished paunch around the middle, he looked like the human inspiration for a Dr. Seuss character.

He was sitting behind his desk, head buried in paperwork, when Wade knocked and stepped into the room.

"Uncle Terry?"

"Wade," his uncle said, taking off his glasses as he came around the desk. "This is quite a surprise."

"Yeah, sorry about that. I should have given you a heads-up.

Especially since I brought friends. It was kind of last-minute."

"No bother," Uncle Terry said. "You're always welcome here."

Wade sensed a "but" in the air. His uncle was always so easy-going, which served as the perfect counterbalance to the chaos and drama of putting on a stage show. But now he seemed awkward, anxious even. Wade sensed he was about to hear the phrase every kid dreads: "We need to talk."

"Is everything okay, Uncle Terry?"

His uncle managed a weak smile as he motioned to one of the club chairs in front of the desk. "Have a seat."

Wade did as he was told.

Uncle Terry sat on the edge of his desk. "Wade, we need to talk."

Crud.

Wade's first thought was that his uncle had somehow found out everything he'd been up to that night. But as any kid who has ever been in trouble before knows, you never guess out loud what you think an adult is going to say.

"Okay," Wade said.

Uncle Terry took a breath. "You really need to settle this situation with your parents."

"Oh," Wade said. For a split second he was relieved, but it didn't last. His uncle was asking him to do something he'd been avoiding for the better part of two years.

"You guys don't want me coming around anymore?" It was a cheap move, but Wade was desperate.

"You know better than that," Uncle Terry scolded. "Roland and I love having you stay with us. In fact, that's a part of the problem."

Wade didn't understand. If he wanted to hang out with Uncle Terry and Roland, and they wanted to hang out with him, and his parents couldn't be bothered anyway, what was the harm?

"I've been selfish, Wade. I've let this go on for far too long. The first time you discovered the glitch in your parents' ridiculous custody arrangement, I should have said something. Maybe I was hoping your folks would figure it out on their own. Or maybe I resented my brother for being so clueless about his son that I never said anything out of spite. Mostly, though, I just didn't want to give up our weekends."

"Then don't."

"It's time, Wade. You have to talk to them. You have to tell them that their arrangement isn't working."

"They won't care. And they won't change. They definitely won't talk to each other. They'll just have their lawyers tweak the algorithm and go back to business as usual."

"They might. They might not. But they're your parents, and they're going to be your parents for a long, long time. At least they deserve the opportunity to correct their mistakes. Most importantly, you need to tell them how you feel. Even if it's messy." Uncle Terry laid a hand on Wade's shoulder. "Especially if it's messy."

Any minute now.

Charley had been saying that to herself ever since they got to the club.

Any minute now Oona is going to come looking for me, because Greg is on the phone and she doesn't want to be the one to tell him where we really are.

Any minute now should have been half an hour ago.

He should have called by now. Or at least texted. He should have checked on her.

She tried to distract herself by watching the show. One of the performers directed her to a choice, out-of-the-way spot in the wings where she could see the whole stage. It was an incredible show, a total blast, but Charley was still miserable.

She couldn't stop thinking about that crack Wade had made on the train. *One way or another, Charley Decker is getting her milkshake tonight.* It had made her so mad. Madder still because deep down she knew he had a point.

And here she was again. She scored the best seat for the coolest show in town and she wasn't enjoying a moment of it. Just like her milkshake at New Farouk's. And like the milkshake, the problem wasn't the show. The problem was her.

Any minute now Greg would call. He had to. But so far, nothing.

There was no way that wasn't bad news.

"She'd barely made it out of the cabaret before the overwhelming feelings of recrimination and shame made her feel nauseous and light-headed. The fresh air helped with the nausea, but that was about it."

Oona sat on the steps outside the stage door. She'd been self-narrating nonstop into Charley's cell phone ever since she left Parker and his sandwich. It usually helped when she was feeling down or confused or overwhelmed. But it wasn't helping now.

"Her mind kept circling back to a quote she read once. She couldn't remember it exactly, but the gist was that most of the harm in the world has been done by people convinced they were absolutely right. She had loved that line, before it had applied to her."

"Oona? You okay, kid?"

Oona turned and saw what was quite possibly the most gorgeous man in the world standing in the doorway. But how did he know her name? It took her a moment, then she put it together. "Eve?"

The man nodded. "It's Steve now," he said, indicating his wardrobe change. He wore jeans and a T-shirt and looked completely different from before, yet Oona felt like she could still see Eve in there as well. Part of her couldn't help think it was unfair that anyone should get to be that beautiful twice.

"Mind if I join you?"

Oona shook her head and Steve sat down next to her on the step. "I couldn't help but overhear a little. Rough night?"

You don't know the half of it, Oona thought.

"I haven't been very nice to someone lately. I thought I knew something about him that made it okay to treat him like that. But I was wrong. I misjudged him, which is bad. But that also means I judged him in the first place, and I kind of pride myself on being above that sort of thing. Why are you smiling?"

"Sorry," Steve said, wiping the grin off his face. "Sounds to me like you're being awfully hard on yourself."

"I deserve it."

"Do you? Everybody gets it wrong sometimes. The world's a

confusing place. The important thing is that you realized your mistake."

"Yeah, well. I don't think he'll see it that way."

"Maybe not. But it's a powerful thing to change the way you think about somebody. Even when they don't change the way they think about you."

Oona startled as the stage door opened.

"There you are," Wade said.

Oona hopped off the steps and backed awkwardly into the alley. If Steve hadn't guessed earlier that she had been talking about Wade, the look on her face made it pretty clear now. "I'm going to head back inside. Give you two a moment," he said. As he passed Wade, he added, "Your uncle was looking for you earlier."

Wade nodded. "He found me."

Steve went inside, leaving Wade and Oona alone on the steps. She was acting funny for some reason. She wouldn't look at him, not directly, and seemed like she had something on her mind but didn't know what to say. And Oona never didn't know what to say.

"What did Steve mean?" Wade asked finally. "About giving us a moment."

She opened her mouth to speak. Then she closed it. Wade

waited. Oona opened her mouth again, and everything in her head came tumbling out.

She told him how she knew about the altercation Wade had with Bryce Spenser in the locker room, only Bryce told her and lots of other people that Wade had used a word that she now knows he didn't use and that's why she was being such a jerk to him lately.

"Huh," Wade said, taking it all in. "What word did he say I used?"

Oona was so worked up that she said it without whispering. Which then made her shriek and cover her mouth.

"Whoa," Wade said. "That's a doozy."

"I know," Oona said. "But then Parker told me what you really said, and why. And now I just hate myself for how I've been treating you."

Wade thought for a long moment. "Is that it?"

"What?"

"Is that the whole story?"

Oona nodded.

"Okay." Wade shrugged. "We're cool. Let's get back inside."

"Wade!"

"What?"

"We're cool? You can't be serious."

"Oona, it's not a big deal."

"It is to me."

"You were sticking up for your friend. I can't knock you for that."

"I know. But I should have been sticking up for you."

"I'm not your friend."

Oona let out a little whimper as her eyes teared up.

"But I'd like to be," Wade added quickly.

Oona shook her head. "You're just saying that so I won't cry."

"I'm really not," Wade said, sitting back down on the steps. Oona remained standing across from him in the alley. "You know, I have to admit a lot of the shots you've been taking at me lately were pretty funny. You got some quality burns in there."

"I said I was sorry," Oona wailed desperately.

Wade laughed. "That's what I like about you, Oona. You're smart and funny and you don't back down, ever. I mean, you will say anything to anybody."

Oona shrugged, heartened but embarrassed by the compliment. "You're the same. The way you stood up for Jason Downey so Bryce would stop picking on him."

"That was no big deal. I don't like Bryce, so calling him out didn't really cost me anything. But you, man. You stand up to people who matter. People you like. Like that poor science teacher in sixth grade . . ."

"Mr. Mathis."

"Right," Wade laughed. "Mr. Mathis. And what about your parents? I can't even bring myself to tell my parents that their ridiculous custody agreement makes me a weekend orphan every four to six weeks. But you fight with your parents when they try to give you an Ursula. You run away from home on principle. And look who was right about that one. Honestly, if anyone should be apologizing, it should be me for making fun of you when you tried to tell us how Alton Peck was an evil corporate supervillain. You totally called it."

Oona shrugged. "That one was pretty obvious."

"Not to me. Or the *New York Times*."

Oona laughed a little as she wiped her eyes with the back of her hand.

"Friends?" Wade said, reaching out.

"Friends," Oona said, taking his hand.

Charley had to call her brother.

The thought made her stomach drop. It didn't make sense, really. She wasn't nervous about him finding out that she'd disobeyed him. For a while she'd even been looking forward to it. But now the idea of *her* having to call *him* and tell him suddenly terrified her.

Of course, there was the distinct possibility that Greg, Marisa, and Mitch were in trouble. That those Woznikowski goons had found them.

Charley's stomach dropped even lower.

"Hey, young lady," a deep, intimidating voice barked behind her. "What do you think you're doing back here?"

Charley whipped around, expecting to see the hulking bouncer, Mickey, looming over her. But it was just Parker, doing another of his voices.

"Sorry," Parker giggled. "Couldn't resist."

Charley said, "Give me your phone."

Parker quickly did as he was told. Charley went into one of the empty dressing rooms and called Greg.

"Who is this?" he answered gruffly.

"Greg?" She could barely hear him. "It's me. Charley. Look, I'm sorry about earlier, and I know you're going to be mad, but there's something I have to tell you . . ."

"Charley?"

"It's just that with you leaving soon, and Mom and Derrick coming back tomorrow, I've been kind of—"

"Charley, I need you to listen carefully."

"Greg, I'm trying to explain—wait. Why are you whispering?"

Five minutes later Charley burst through the stage doors to find Wade and Oona sitting on the steps.

"There you are," she said, gasping for breath.

"Charley?" Oona said. "Is everything okay?"

"Well," Charley began, "we have good news. And we have bad news. Really bad news."

EIGHT

"What about this one?" Oona asked, holding up a slinky blue dress with spaghetti straps and lace stitching down one side. "For Greg?"

Wade looked the dress over. "Nah. That's a size eight. With his hips we won't get him in anything smaller than a ten. Maybe a twelve."

Oona went back to looking through the stacks.

Once Charley had gathered her friends, she'd filled them in on her call with Greg. The good news was that Greg, Marisa, and Mitch had managed to get Mitch's Ursula from the locker at Fun Never Stops.

"What's the bad news?" Wade had asked.

"The Woznikowski brothers are there, too."

"No way," said Oona. "How'd those bruisers know where to find them?"

Charley shrugged. "I don't know, but they're staking out the exits. Greg, Marisa, and Mitch barely had time to duck into the bathrooms before they were spotted."

"So they've got the Ursula," Wade said, "but they're all trapped in the john?"

"Pretty much," Charley said.

"We have to help them," Oona said.

"No doubt," Parker chimed in. "Any ideas? Because I've got squat."

Charley scanned the dressing room. "I think I have an idea," she said.

"Dude," Parker said, after she told them what she was thinking. "That's wild."

Oona gave him a look.

"What? Look, I know I say it a lot. But it *really* fits here."

"It could work," Wade said. Then he led the others back to the storage rooms where his uncle kept all the old props and costumes. He and Oona started going through the dresses, while Parker and Charley went next door to rummage through the wigs.

So far Wade had found a poodle skirt and pink angora sweater combo for Mitch, and settled on a tux for Marisa.

"How about this one?" Oona said.

"Whoa." Wade blinked. The dress Oona held up by the hanger was a backless, bright pink evening gown with bouffant skirt complete with English netting and a halter neck. It wasn't just a statement dress, it was a full-fledged fashion manifesto.

"Too much, right?" Oona asked, about to put it back on the rack. "You can probably see this dress from space."

Wade slowly nodded his head. "That might work for us. We want people to notice the dress. Think about it: If you're looking at the dress . . ."

Oona picked it up. "You're not looking at the face."

"Exactly."

Wade and Oona loaded the clothes into a garment bag just as Charley and Parker came in with their wig options. Wade picked a brunette, medium bob with bangs for Mitch and went big and blonde for Greg. He'd just slick Marisa's hair back with product.

"Makeup?" Wade said as they headed out.

"I lifted some samples from the dressing room," Oona said.

"Okay. I think we're good to go."

"So, Francisco," Oona said. "What do you think the media gets right, and what does it get wrong, about the gig economy?"

Oona hadn't let up since they got in the car. In the last few minutes she had managed to extract enough information from their poor Lyft driver to fill a book. He was a senior at UIC, where he was studying criminal justice. He lived off campus with three of his buddies in a four-story brownstone on South Racine Avenue across from the firehouse. Yes, he planned on staying in Chicago after he graduated. No, he wasn't opposed to leaving the city if job opportunities presented themselves elsewhere.

It was a little annoying at first, but then Charley figured out that she was probably talking nonstop so he couldn't think too much about what he was doing driving four seventh graders around the South Loop in the dead of night.

"Um," poor Francisco said as he pulled into the arcade parking lot. "Here we are."

The boys jumped out of the car. Wade carried the garment bag and Parker had the duffel with the wigs, shoes, and makeup. The girls were about fifty yards behind because Oona had stopped to show Francisco that they'd be giving him the full, five-star rating for his service tonight.

She and Charley were hurrying through the parking lot to catch up with the boys, when Charley stopped suddenly, grabbing Oona and pulling her behind a large SUV.

"What gives?" Oona asked, concerned.

"I need you to hide me," Charley said. "Keep walking."

The girls moved in lockstep through the parking lot.

"On your left. About ten o'clock. See the big guy in the flannel?"

"The one cracking his knuckles?"

"Uh-huh. That's one of the guys from New Farouk's."

"The Wozni-whatsit brothers?"

"I think so," Charley said. She kind of doubted he would recognize her, but she wanted Oona to block her view of the guy anyway so he wouldn't recognize Charley recognizing him.

She breathed a big sigh of relief when they made it safely inside the arcade. "The other one is probably in here somewhere."

Oona concurred. "We need to hurry."

"Well, well, well," the girls heard a loud, mocking voice behind them. "Look who it is."

Charley sighed, "Aw, crumbs."

The girls watched as four obnoxiously aggressive guys shoved their way through the crowd, the leader pointing an accusing finger and shouting, "Stay right there, missy. I mean it, now."

"You know them?"

"Remember those aggro-bros I told you about earlier? In the convenience store."

"That's them?"

"Uh-huh."

"I hate Illinois aggro-bros," Oona said. "What do we do?"

Charley didn't know. There were a lot of people around; they could call for help. But that would get security involved, maybe even the police. Not to mention any commotion would attract the attention of the looming Woznikowski brothers.

Charley thought for a minute. "Call Wade."

Oona pulled Charley's phone out of her pocket. "What should I say?"

"Nothing. Just keep the line open so he can hear."

"You have a plan?" Oona said hopefully.

Charley wasn't sure she'd go that far.

"Fancy seeing you again," Puka said as he and his pals surrounded Charley and Oona.

"Yeah," Charley said. "Small world, huh?"

"It is a small world," Puka said, as if this were somehow a sick burn. "And it's going to get smaller. See, after we left the convenience store, my crew and me, we did some thinking."

"Yeah, we did," one of the Camo Pants chimed in, high-fiving the other two bros.

"Uh-huh. And that guy you and your brother were going on about?"

Charley nodded. "Billy Russo?"

"Him, right. Well, we think you and your brother made him up."

"Oh, do you now?"

"Yeah, that wasn't cool!" Camo Pants huffed indignantly. "Not. Cool. At. All."

Charley couldn't believe these guys. Their feelings were actually hurt. Four hours ago they were about to beat up some poor guy in a convenience store just because they really didn't have anything else better to do. But the real injustice here was that they'd been tricked out of doing it. Talk about thin skin.

"Wait, wait," Charley said with a *hold on* wave of her hands. "You don't believe Billy is real? Billy Russo? Seriously?"

Oona blinked nervously. Charley's plan, as far as she had been able to explain it, was to follow her lead. Oona wasn't sure what that was, but did the best she could.

"Billy is going to laugh when he hears this," she chimed in. "Not real? Billy Russo? You guys really think he doesn't exist?"

"That's what we said. Are you deaf?"

"No, I'm Oona. And you are?"

"Dirk," Puka snorted. "What's it to you?"

"Okay, Dirk," Charley said crisply. "Would you like to meet Billy Russo? Because he's here."

"Here?"

"Yep. Billy Russo is here. In the arcade," Charley said with so much confidence that Oona herself was beginning to believe the guy actually existed. "We can settle this right now, Dirk. It's your call. What do you want to do?"

"Who is it?" Parker asked.

"Charley and Oona," Wade said, phone pressed tightly to his ear. "But they're talking to someone else." Wade listened carefully, concern growing on his face.

"Did they butt-dial you?"

"I don't think so," Wade said, holding out his phone so Parker could hear, too. "I think they ran into those jerks Charley was telling us about from the convenience store. I think they're in trouble."

The boys listened as Charley and Oona rambled on about guys named "Dirk" and "Billy Russo."

"I do not get what she's trying to do," Wade said, equal parts worried and flummoxed.

"I think I know," Parker said.

"You do?"

"Here," Parker said, handing the duffel bag to Wade. "Take the costumes and find Greg and the others. I'll handle this."

"You sure?"

Parker drummed his belly and gave Wade a cocked finger gun. "I got this."

NINE

2:15 A.M.

Parker stopped about twenty feet from the arcade's help desk. He lowered his head, closed his eyes, and shook his arms loosely at his sides. He took a deep breath, held it, looked up, and let it out slowly. He was ready.

"All right, Parker," he said to himself. "Time to bring the magic."

As he made his way to the help desk, he started sucking on his lower lip and breathing rapidly. The guy behind the desk was, according to his name tag, Eugene.

Poor Eugene had no idea what he was in for.

"Machinestolemydollar!" Parker bellowed, kicking the side of the desk.

"Hey," Eugene said. "Please don't do that."

"Machinestolemydollar!" Parker repeated, louder, pointing to a nearby soda machine.

"Okay, calm down," Eugene said. "You're saying the soda machine took your dollar?"

Parker nodded frantically.

"I'm sorry, but we don't—"

"MACHINESTOLEMY—"

"Eugene! What the heck's going on here?" The security guard, Randy, looked wearily from Eugene to Parker.

"Soda machine ate his dollar. He wants it back. I tried to tell him—"

"MACHINE—"

"Shut it!" Randy the guard barked at Parker.

Parker started to blink frantically the way little kids do when they're trying not to cry.

"Aw, great," Randy groaned.

"Kid," Eugene said, tagging in. "Who did you come here with? Do you have a grown-up with you?"

Parker shrugged. "Just Dirk. Dirk the Jerk."

"Okay, good. Who's Dirk?"

"He's my sister's boyfriend. He brought me here with his jerk friends so she could study for her AP exams. He's a jerk and I hate him. He smokes cigarettes and blows in my face when my sister's not looking, but my mom and dad say that she's just going through her bad boy phase and that it will pass, but I don't think so and you know what ... you know what ... you know what?"

"What, kid?"

"MACHINESTOLEMYDOLLAR!!!!!!"

Everyone in the general vicinity of the help desk stopped what they were doing and looked over at Parker. Which, of course, was the general idea.

Randy said, "We need to find this Dirk guy."

"I'll page him," Eugene said. "Hey, kid. What's your name?"

"Billy. Billy Russo."

Two more security guards hustled over to the help desk.

"What in the world is going on over here?"

The temptation to answer with his new catchphrase was nearly overwhelming, but Parker remembered that the quiet moments make a performance, too.

"We need to find this kid's people," Randy said. "Pronto." He turned to Parker. "Okay, kid? Kid?"

"Billy," Eugene added helpfully.

"Billy. I need you to calm down now. This guy you're with, Dirk?"

"Dirk the Jerk."

"Sure. Dirk the Jerk. Can you describe him and his friends so we can find them for you?"

Parker started to huff and pace back and forth as the men at the help desk braced for another tantrum. But he was really just looking for Charley, Oona, and the convenience store aggro-bros.

Once he spotted Charley sizing up a guy in a telltale puka shell necklace over by the entrance, he stopped huffing and pacing and said, calmly, "Sure. I can do that."

"He's really here?"

"That's what we said," Charley answered. "Still sure you want to meet him?"

Camo Pants looked warily at Puka (aka Dirk, aka Dirk the Jerk). "I thought they made him up."

"They did make him up!" Puka (aka Dirk, aka Dirk the Jerk) insisted desperately.

Charley and Oona just shrugged and smiled at each other knowingly.

"You made him up," Puka (aka Dirk, aka Dirk the Jerk) tried again. "Both of you."

At that moment, an announcement came over the PA system:

"Hi, everybody. I'm here with Billy Russo, who's looking for his friend Dirk. Dirk, could you please come meet Billy at the help desk right away."

"No way . . ." Camo Pants said quietly as the color drained from his face. The other two convenience store aggro-bros started backing away slowly toward the door.

"Nah." Puka (aka Dirk, aka Dirk the Jerk) shook his head violently. "Nah. I still don't buy it." He pointed a shaky finger at the girls. "You're . . . you're lying. There is no Billy Russo!"

"Excuse me, sir? Is your name Dirk?"

Puka (aka Dirk, aka Dirk the Jerk) turned slowly toward the two security guards. "Yes?"

"Oh, great. Look, we have a situation here. Billy is really losing it. Can you come with us, please?"

All four of the convenience store aggro-bros were through the doors and into the parking lot somewhere between "with" and "us."

The two guards watched blankly. Then one of them said, "Maybe we should just give the kid his stupid dollar."

Mitch Rosenfeld looked at himself in the full-length mirrors that lined the hallway outside the arcade bathrooms. He smoothed down his poodle skirt and fussed with his bangs.

"Leave the wig alone," Wade admonished.

"This is wrong," he said. "This is so, so messed up."

"Dude," Wade said. "I get that this isn't your thing. But that doesn't make it—"

"No, no," Mitch said, staring intently into the mirror. "That's not what I meant. I just . . . man, I look like my mom."

Wade didn't know about that, but he was pretty pleased with his work, if he did say so himself. Mitch wasn't going to win any beauty contests, but Wade had done those cheekbones justice.

Marisa came out of the women's restroom in the tux, her hair slicked back and shiny. She still wore her Chuck Taylors, though, which made the whole look even cooler. Wade gave her the duffel bag and she put her street clothes inside.

"Where's Greg?" she said.

"Still primping," Wade said.

Just then, Greg came out of the bathroom. Wade had to give him credit; he'd really committed. The exploding, high-voltage pink dress, the towering, blonde helmet of a wig, the eighties-throwback-Glamour-Shots makeup, the wedge heels—Greg was working it all.

He fidgeted awkwardly with his décolletage. "What?"

"Nothing," Marisa said quickly. "You look . . . great."

"Yeah?"

Marisa went to hand the duffel back to Wade.

"Actually," Greg said to Marisa. "You probably ought to hold on to that. The Ursula's in there, too."

"Really?" Mitch said doubtfully. "Is that a good idea?"

"You and Greg are both in low heels," Wade reminded Mitch. "And Marisa here was all-city in the four hundred meter."

"I didn't know you were a fan," Marisa teased.

Wade coughed awkwardly. "Charley must have told me," he mumbled.

"Point is," Greg explained, "that if our little disguises don't work, one of us is going to have to make a break for it with the Ursula. Marisa's our best bet in that department."

"What happens to us, then?" Mitch said, trying to keep his voice steady.

Wade shrugged. "I guess it's going to get pretty crowded in that trunk."

Mitch's knees wobbled under his poodle skirt.

Greg gave Wade a look, then he said, "Let's try to think positive. The Woznikowski brothers are going to be looking for one person, not three."

"Let alone three people looking this fabulous," Marisa chimed in.

"Exactly," Greg said. "Wade, find Charley and the others and meet us at the car. We'll be a couple of minutes behind you."

"Got it."

It only took a couple of minutes for Wade to spot Charley and Oona and tell them it was time to leave.

"We need to get Parker first," Charley said. "He's over at the help desk."

Wade looked over at Parker, surrounded by three security guards who looked more scared of him than he was of them.

"Oi!" Wade yelled in Parker's direction.

"Oh, and call him 'Billy.'"

"Billy!" Wade yelled. "Let's motor."

Parker, who had kept the help desk in a state of anxious anticipation lest he have another meltdown, turned and said, "Thanks, guys. Have a nice night."

"I'm confused. Should we just let him go like that?" Eugene asked the group.

Randy said, "Absolutely."

Heel to toe, heel to toe, heel to toe.

Marisa's last-minute advice to the guys was running like a mantra through Greg's head as they walked carefully through the arcade. In a way, navigating the heels was a blessing, because it kept them all, especially Mitch, from suspiciously dashing for the exits. The guys had no choice but to take it slow.

Marisa clocked one of the Woznikowski brothers over by the Skee-Ball games.

"That one of them?" she asked Mitch.

Mitch whimpered in the affirmative.

But the man barely looked their way, and didn't give them a second glance.

"One down," Greg said quietly.

As they made it to the main doors, Greg started to feel more nervous. They hadn't spotted the other brother yet, which gave Greg the uneasy sensation that the man was sneaking up from behind.

Then Greg spotted him through the glass doors. He stood just outside the arcade, guarding the entrance and blocking their path to the parking lot.

And he was looking right at them.

"What do we do?" Mitch croaked.

"Just ignore him," Greg said. Up ahead, he glimpsed Charley and the others already in the parking lot, crouched down behind the Mustang, watching. They were so close to getting away . . .

Then he had an idea. His first thought had been to give the second Woznikowski a wide berth, to walk as far away from him as possible. But that might encourage the guy to watch them go.

Instead, Greg started walking *toward* him.

"What are you doing?" Marisa trilled in a singsongy voice.

"Trust me," Greg intoned back.

The second Woznikowski stared at the trio for a minute that seemed to last a lifetime. Then, as Greg had gambled, he started to ever so subtly back away, giving them room to pass him on their way to the parking lot.

But Greg kept drifting closer to the other Woznikowski.

"Greg, honey," Marisa said through clenched teeth. "I love you, but you're playing a dangerous game."

Charley and her friends held their collective breath as they watched Greg, Marisa, and Mitch approach the Woznikowski twin perched at the edge of the parking lot.

It looked like smooth sailing. Until . . .

"What is your brother doing?" Oona whispered.

Charley watched as Greg drifted closer to the flanneled kidnapper. When he was less than ten feet away, Greg looked out into the parking lot, locked eyes with Charley, and smiled.

She knew that smile.

"Oh no," Charley groaned.

"What?" Oona said.

Greg was . . . well, he was a shortstop. It was arguably the hardest position in baseball. Balls were always coming at them fast and hard, and they needed to be cool with that. Like it, even. To play shortstop well, a person needed ice water in their veins, catlike reflexes, and a certain disregard for their own safety.

In other words, they had to be a little nuts.

"Greg. He's going to do something."

"What? What's he going to do?"

Charley had no idea, only that it would be stupid and danger-ous. Greg picked up the pace and wobbled erratically, like a newborn fawn with an inner-ear infection (which, unfortu-nately, also had the effect of tilting his wig just slightly off-kilter). The drape of his hot pink dress caught the glint from the parking lot lights, practically illuminating him as he tee-tered closer, closer to the Woznikowski twin. Oh, god.

"Hey, buddy!" Greg called as he stumbled up to the big man with as much grace as he could muster. "Got a light?"

"We are so dead," Parker eeked.

The big dude turned, looking Greg up and down. "You don't have a cigarette."

"Oh, yeah," Greg said, patting his dress in a ridiculous search for pockets. "Can I bum one of those, too?"

"Sweetie," Marisa chided, sidling up beside Greg and locking one arm, forcefully, in his. Her other arm was busy propping up a trembling Mitch, who looked ready to either faint or run away. "You know you don't even smoke."

"I know, sugar. But no time like the present, right?"

Marisa, in an impressive display of strength and leverage, yanked Greg away.

"Oh, well," Greg called as his girlfriend dragged him across the parking lot. "Maybe next time. Thanks anyway, buddy!"

The Woznikowski brother just shook his head and returned his attention to the arcade entrance.

"I think I'm going to throw up," Wade said when they were in the clear.

"Get in line," Parker croaked.

Greg, Marisa, and Mitch had an uneventful journey back to the Mustang.

"You're insane!" Mitch screeched at Greg as he tossed the duffel bag in the trunk. "I mean, what was that all about?"

Charley looked at her brother. She knew exactly what that was all about.

"Payback," she said. "That was for me, wasn't it? For disobeying you when you said to just go home."

Greg tapped his nose and got in the car. Marisa and Mitch sat up front with him, while Charley and her friends crammed into the back.

"Okay," Greg said. "We got the Ursula. Now what do we do with it?"

"Oona and I are on it," Charley said. "Oona?"

Oona, ear pressed to Charley's phone, held up one finger. "No, no, the car's fine. Uh-huh. Listen, this is going to sound kind of strange but . . . want to help us take down Alton Peck? Strike a blow against the tech uprising? You do? Cool."

Oona looked up from Charley's phone. "Michaela's in."

"The girl from the impound lot?" Wade said.

"She's a tech wiz," Charley explained. "Maybe she'll know what to do with the Ursula."

"Okay," Greg said, satisfied. "Rogers Park it is. Again." He took off his heels before starting the car. But Marisa stopped him when he went to take off the wig, too.

"Keep it on," she said.

"Really?"

"You just . . ." she sighed, throwing in a wistful flutter of the eyes. "You never get dolled up for me anymore."

Greg laughed and started up the car. "Anything for you, big daddy."

"You know what I can't figure out," Marisa said as they drove up the highway. "Is how those flannel guys—"

"The Woznikowski brothers."

"Yeah, them. I can't figure out how they found us at the arcade so quickly."

"I've been wondering about that, too," Greg said.

"Maybe they knew that's where I hid the Ursula," Mitch suggested.

"Maybe," Charley said. "But if they knew that, they would have gotten the Ursula *before* they abducted you. The Ursula is the proof, that's what they really need. You're just a loose end. No offense."

"Uh-huh."

"Besides," Greg said, "we beat them to the arcade. By a while. In fact, they didn't arrive until after we got the Ursula and were trying to leave."

"Which means they didn't tail us there, either," Marisa said.

"So, if they didn't tail you," Charley said, "and they didn't know where you were going, how did they follow you?"

"I don't know," Marisa said. "But however they did it, we better figure it out before they do it again."

TEN

Greg pulled into the convenience store parking lot across the street from Daftari's Towing and Impound. Michaela had told them to meet her there after Oona had explained how the Woznikowskis kept showing up wherever they went. She was waiting in front with a small metal box in her hands.

"Do you have your Pangea ID tag on you?" she asked Mitch the second he stepped out of the car. If she even noticed he was in an angora sweater and a poodle skirt, it didn't register on her face. She was all business.

"Um, yeah?"

"Can I see it, please?"

Mitch fished his ID tag out of the duffel bag and handed it to her. Michaela brought it over to the front of the Mustang. She put the metal box on the hood and opened it. The box was lined with soundproofing foam. Inside were an X-Acto knife, a lead magnet, and duct tape. She laid these all out carefully on the hood as well. Except the X-Acto knife, which she kept in her hand.

"Wait," Mitch said nervously. "What are you doing?"

"I'm dissecting your ID tag."

"But," Mitch sputtered, "that will ruin it."

"So?" Wade scoffed.

"It's just, they're a real pain to replace. The IT guys give you a lot of hassle about it."

"Dude?" Parker guffawed. "You don't really think you still work there?"

Mitch shrugged. "Well, I don't know."

"They drugged you and threw you in a trunk!" Wade exclaimed.

"I know! But they have dental. And profit sharing."

"And kidnapping!"

"You just wait until you guys have to navigate this job market!"

"Guys," Michaela cut in. "Take a look at this."

She had peeled back the laminate on Mitch's ID tag and removed his picture, revealing a computer chip that was the length, width, and thickness of a postage stamp.

Charley spoke for everyone when she said, "Well, that can't be good."

"It's a tracking chip," Michaela said. "Meant for short-range surveillance. Probably just in there to keep an eye on the employees during working hours. Make sure no one's sneaking off with proprietary technology."

"Or the copier toner," Parker added.

"That's how they did it?" Greg said. "That's how they've been following us?"

"Yep."

"But I thought you said the chip was for short-range surveillance."

Michaela tossed Mitch's ID tag into the metal box. "Yeah, but if you know what you're doing and you have a strong enough receiver, you can boost the signal up to about forty miles. Maybe more." Michaela closed the box and duct-taped the magnet to the lid.

"And that will block the signal?"

"Probably."

Mitch's voice cracked a little. "Only probably?"

Michaela said, "It should be fine."

"Why don't we just destroy it?" Marisa suggested.

"We can, sure. But you never know. It might be useful."

"Okay," Greg said, pointing at the box. "But if that thing starts humming like the Ark of the Covenant, I get to pound it into little pieces."

Now that the tracking chip had been disabled, Greg and the others could safely bring the Mustang into the impound lot.

"Wait," Charley said to Michaela. "What about your dad?"

Michaela pointed to the office window, where they could see a very contented Mr. Daftari fast asleep in the chair behind the counter.

"Don't worry about him," Michaela said, leading them around the office. "He's out like a light, just as long as no one opens the door and trips the shopkeeper's bell."

Michaela led the group back to a long, freestanding brick building that was divided into four separate garages. Three had cars in them, but the one closest to the office was set up like a personal work space. Two long tables took up the center of this garage, each littered with computer and electronic equipment in varying states of disassembly. Against the wall was a desk with a massive computer system all booted up and waiting for them.

Greg and Mitch changed back into their street clothes while

Charley and Oona filled Michaela in on everything that had happened since they left the impound lot.

"Well," she said, putting Mitch's Ursula down on the desk. "You guys sure have been busy. All I've done since you left is some light reading and a few games of backgammon with my dad."

"We like to make the most of our weekends," Charley quipped.

"No doubt," Michaela said, hooking the Ursula up to a hard drive about the size of a standard piece of luggage.

"What we need to do now," Charley said, "is get the information about the many crimes of Alton Peck off this Ursula and then figure out how to get it to the proper authorities."

"Which will be extra challenging because Alton Peck has about half of the proper authorities in his pocket," Oona added.

"Right. That, too."

Michaela thought for a minute. "Okay," she said. "I think it's time to take a look at this Ursula."

Ten minutes later, Michaela looked up for the first time and said, "Huh."

Never before had such an innocuous word managed to sound so ominous.

After Michaela finished downloading the hard drive from Mitch's Ursula onto her server, she had started to carefully take apart and dissect the black obelisk, which was now laid out neatly across one of the tables. Everyone else in the room had come to the unspoken agreement that the best thing they could do was keep quiet while she worked.

"Can you maybe be more specific?" asked Parker.

Michaela pinched her nose under her glasses. "Things are much, much worse than I thought."

"Sure. That clears it up, thanks."

Everyone gathered around the bench while Michaela explained. "See that piece there? That's the reason why Mitch's Ursula linked up with Alton Peck's."

"So, you found the glitch."

"Oh, I found it," Michaela said. "But it's not a glitch."

"I don't follow," Wade said.

"It's a feature, not a bug," Charley said, catching on.

"Exactly. Or, rather, it will be eventually."

"I'm sorry," Wade said, speaking for most of them. "But the more you explain, the more confused I get."

"Every Ursula is designed to sync up with a kind of central, host terminal that will collect and store all its data."

"It's called the Mother Ursula," Mitch said. "And it is *massive*. Takes up the first five floors of Pangea headquarters. Pretty much runs the whole company."

Michaela made a face. "Mother Ursula?"

"Hey, I didn't name it," Mitch said.

"Anyway," Michaela resumed, "that's what this piece is for—it will link this Ursula to your Mother Ursula. That's the feature. But the Mother Ursula can't link with all the . . . *baby* Ursulas yet."

"Why not?" Charley asked.

Oona snapped her fingers. "Satellites. That's why Pangea keeps sending up so many satellites. Peck needs them so that all the Ursulas can send their data to the Mother Ursula."

"How many satellites are we talking about?" Marisa asked.

Michaela chewed her finger for a moment. "Conservatively? I'd say about five, maybe six, hundred."

Wade said, "I'm guessing that's a lot?"

"Let's put it this way," Michaela said. "China only has around two hundred eighty."

"Wait. All of China?"

Michaela nodded.

"Okay," Greg said. "What happens when Peck finally gets all his satellites up in the sky?"

"The baby Ursulas will all link up to the Mother Ursula. As designed. But until then, they have nowhere to send their data. Which is why, if two of them get close enough to each other . . ."

"Like Mitch's did with Alton Peck's—"

"They sync up with each other. That's the bug part."

"Any port in a storm," Charley said.

"Kind of, yeah."

"My guess is that Peck has timed it so that once the Ursula goes on sale worldwide, those satellites will all be up and running and linked with the Mother Ursula. That's what I'd do," Michaela said reasonably.

"Monday," Wade said. "That's when the Ursula goes on sale."

Charley stared at the disassembled black obelisk on the table. "You guys are saying that, in two days' time, anyone who buys an Ursula is going to have all their data collected in space, for Pangea to use, or sell, or manipulate however they want."

Michaela nodded. "Only not just their data. Everything about them."

Wade gulped. "Everything?"

"Everything. Take a look at this," she said, handing a piece of motherboard to Wade. "That's for recording video and audio."

"Okay," Wade said.

"It never shuts off."

Wade dropped the piece on the table like a hot potato.

"Whoa, whoa, hold on," Marisa said. "You're saying that an Ursula is always recording?"

"Sound *and* picture. As soon as people start putting Ursulas in their homes, personal privacy as we know it becomes virtually—pardon the pun—extinct. Everything you say, do, write, read, watch, hear—will all instantly become the property of Alton Peck."

Wade gave Oona a nudge. "Well, Oona. If anyone ever deserved to say 'I told you so' . . .'"

Oona shook her head. "Please. I've never wanted to be wrong so badly in my life."

"We need to get this to somebody," Greg said, pointing warily at the Ursula.

"Yeah, but who?" Mitch despaired. "Alton Peck has thrown a lot of money around Washington. It won't be easy finding someone who isn't in his pocket."

"Oona," Charley said.

"On it," Oona said, plopping down at one of Michaela's many computers to start scouring the internet.

Meanwhile, Greg walked over to the workbench and picked up the lockbox with the magnet taped on top.

"Michaela? If I take Mitch's ID tag out of the lockbox, will it start sending a signal again?"

"Yeah," Michaela said. "You don't want to do that."

Charley was catching on to her brother's train of thought. "Or do we?"

Michaela got it now, too. "Okay, sure. But that chip will start transmitting immediately. The minute you open the box, you're gonna need to get as far away from it as possible, as fast as possible."

Greg smiled. "I can do fast."

Just then, Oona's fingers stopped their furious clicking on the keyboard.

"Guys," she said. "I found something. Well, more like some*one*."

"Someone we can give the Ursula to?"

Oona nodded. "You're not going to believe this."

They all rushed over to take a look.

"Indiana Senator Gabriela Zelzah?" Charley said, reading off the monitor. The name sounded vaguely familiar.

"She's perfect," Oona continued. "She's on the Senate Intelligence Committee, and she's never taken a dime from Alton Peck or Pangea."

"And you think we can trust her?"

"Scroll down to the picture."

"The one where she's shaking hands with the president?"

"Uh-huh. Now look at the person on the other side of her."

Standing beside the senator was an awkward young man who looked lost. Charley squinted. Was that? Nah, it couldn't be.

"It is," Oona giggled, reading her best friend's mind. "I double-checked. That's Oscar. Oscar *Zelzah*."

"Wait, you mean our Oscar?" Greg said. "The wayward fraternity pledge from the convenience store?"

Everyone crowded closer for a better look. Charley remembered how freaked out Oscar's fraternity brothers had been when he returned. How Oscar had to call his mom right away and tell her not to call the governor of Illinois. Charley had thought he was just exaggerating. Apparently not.

Charley remembered something else. Oscar Zelzah owed her a favor.

ELEVEN

4:10 A.M.

When Charley called Oscar, he was eating pancakes at an all-night diner halfway between campus and O'Hare airport. The other pledges and half the fraternity brothers were there, too. And every one of them was keeping a close eye on Oscar to make sure they didn't lose him again.

"Charley?" Oscar said into his phone. "I'm just eating pancakes. What are you doing?"

Oscar listened quietly for several minutes.

"Hold on. He was in your trunk the whole time?" Oscar finally said when Charley was done explaining everything. "No, I know. It's just—uh-huh. Of course, I'll call her now. You just sit tight. Okay, talk to you soon."

He hung up and stared at his plate of half-eaten pancakes. His mom was going to freak out. Which, of course, wasn't the big takeaway here. There were seriously big issues at play tonight, fate-of-the-world stuff. But all Oscar could think was how, after tonight, his mom would probably homeschool him until he was thirty.

Oscar called Charley back ten minutes later.

"He says to sit tight," Charley told the group after she hung up. "His mom's getting on a jet as we speak."

"Out of Washington?" Oona asked.

Charley shook her head. "She's in Indianapolis for a fundraiser."

"That puts her about an hour's flight to Chicago," Marisa reasoned. "Then however long it takes to get here. I'd say we're looking at two hours, at least."

"I'll bust out some popcorn," Michaela said amiably. "We can put on a movie. Any of you guys like sci-fi?"

"Actually, I need to run a little errand," Greg said.

"But the senator mom said to sit tight," Parker protested.

"Two hours is a long time. I can't just sit around and hope that Alton Peck and his goons don't find us in the meantime."

"How would they?" Wade said. "I mean, we blocked the signal."

"True," Michaela said clinically. "But not before it gave your last location as the convenience store across the street."

"Michaela's right," Greg said. "That's way too close for comfort. We need to give them somewhere else to look."

"What did you have in mind?" Marisa asked, though her tone suggested she already knew.

"I'm going to use Mitch's ID tag to create a little misdirection."

"You don't need me for that, do you?" Mitch hoped out loud.

"Wow, heart of a lion right there," Parker quipped.

"Hey! You get drugged and thrown in the trunk of a car for four hours and see what it does for your nerves!"

"Okay, okay," Greg called for order. "Everyone pipe down. The rest of you stay here. I'm just taking Charley."

"Why her?" Mitch said.

"Because she'll just invent a reason to follow him anyway," Marisa said, matter-of-factly. "At least this way he can keep an eye on her."

"Keep an eye on me?" Charley protested.

"In that case, you should probably bring Wade with you, too," Oona reasoned.

"Seriously?" Charley exclaimed, irritated that they were talking about her rather than to her.

And also because they weren't wrong.

Wade stepped out of the bathroom to find Oona standing by the door.

"Oh, sorry," he said. "You waiting to get in?"

Oona shook her head. "Are you scared?" she asked as they started walking together out to the car.

"Yeah," he said. "I am. Are you?"

Oona nodded. "I wish I was going with you guys."

"No, you don't."

A nervous laugh slipped out of her mouth. "You're right. I don't."

Wade gave her a look. In a strange way, seeing how clearly worried she was for him actually made him feel better, more confident. Out of all the insanely improbable things that had happened tonight, becoming friends with Oona Adair was definitely at the top of the list. That must count for something. "We'll be fine," he said reassuringly.

"Will you do something for me, though?"

"Sure."

"Get out your phone."

Wade did as he was told. She then had him activate the share location feature so she could track them. "I know I'm probably overreacting," she said.

"No, it's a good idea."

Greg and Michaela joined them. Michaela had the lockbox in her hand.

"Once you take the tag out of the box, it will go live. Immediately." She handed the box to Greg. "I can't stress this enough."

"Got it," he said. He looked at Wade. "You ready?"

"Oh. I suppose."

Charley was waiting for the others by the Mustang. She was not pouting. She just wanted a moment by herself. To, well, pout.

The irony of the situation was not lost on her. All night she'd been trying to get Greg to notice her, to spend time with her. To pick her just one time. And now that he had, it felt even worse. He wasn't bringing her and Wade along because he wanted to. He was only doing it so he could keep an eye on her. This wasn't what she'd wanted.

"Hey, there," Marisa said. "You okay?"

Charley set her jaw. "I'm fine," she said. It came out sharper than she meant, which made her feel bad. Try as she might, she didn't really dislike Marisa. And, if Charley were being honest, Marisa was a lot more patient with Charley than Charley would have been with her had it been the other way around. Not that she'd ever admit that out loud, of course.

"You think this is a bad idea," Charley said after a lull. "Don't you?"

Marisa thought about it. "I don't know. There is a certain strategy to it. But you know your brother. He always has to keep moving. Especially whenever he gets nervous or scared."

Charley gave her brother's girlfriend a curious look. "Greg never gets scared," Charley said. "I mean, at least not before tonight."

Marisa laughed, but not unkindly. "Sure, he does. He gets frightened all the time. He's terrified about graduating, starting college. Moving away."

"But he wants to do all that."

"He does. But it still scares him. Why do you think he's always on the go lately? It's so he doesn't have to stop and think about what's next. I know you see it, too. The way he always has to be out doing something. Move, move, move. Gets exhausting, doesn't it? Take earlier tonight. I didn't want to go out after

New Farouk's. I wanted to stay at the house and watch movies with you guys."

"You did?"

"Absolutely," Marisa said. "And deep down, I know Greg did, too."

"Then why didn't he?"

"Maybe because it's the kind of thing he's going to miss when he's gone." Marisa shrugged. "Look, all I know is that lately he has to keep himself distracted, or else he starts getting really antsy."

"Like at the impound lot," Charley said, remembering. "When he had to sit in the waiting room while you came to get the money."

"Exactly," Marisa said. "That just about killed him. Because he finally had to stop and think. Not just about losing the car, but about everything, you know?"

"Know what?" Greg said as he approached the car with Wade.

"Nothing," Charley said quickly.

"You okay?" Wade said quietly to Charley.

Charley didn't rightfully know. Hearing Marisa talk that way about her brother had rattled her. It was easier when Greg was just being clueless and lovestruck. To think that maybe, deep down, he was also afraid, not just about the car, but the future as well? That frightened *her*. Even when he was being an idiot, her brother had still always made her feel safe. Had that all been a lie? And if so, who was doing the lying? Was he lying to her? Or was she lying to herself?

"Charley?" Wade prodded.

"Huh? Oh, yeah," she covered. "All good."

They got in the car: Charley in the front with Greg, Wade in the back with the lockbox.

Michaela opened the back gate to the impound lot, which led onto an easy-to-miss alley, and told Greg which side streets to take to get back to the highway.

"It might take a little longer, but it will keep you off the main avenues, just in case those twins are in the area."

"Thank you," Charley said. "For everything."

Greg followed her instructions to the highway. Ten minutes later, he said, "Okay. Do it."

Wade opened the lockbox and took out Mitch's ID tag.

They were now, officially, bait.

TWELVE

5:18 A.M.

Alton Peck paced angrily across his penthouse office. But then Alton Peck did pretty much everything angrily. For a guy who had everything he'd ever wanted—money, fame, success—he still wasn't happy. Because to him, happiness was less about what he had and more about what other people no longer had—because he had it.

Basically, Alton Peck was a sore winner.

Case in point: this other Mustang.

In the next two days Peck had to get the last of his satellites online and an Ursula in every home. Then he had to steal the privacy of billions of people and become the richest and most powerful man in the history of the world. It wasn't easy. And, to top it all off, he had to help the morons find that runaway accountant—a task that had gotten a lot harder ever since the tracker in the accountant's ID tag had suddenly gone dark.

But all Alton Peck could think about was that other Mustang. The Woznikowskis insisted that they had put the accountant in the trunk of *his* Mustang. And although they were morons, they did know cars. It wasn't like them to mistake one year and model of Mustang for another.

But if they were right, that meant there was another Skyway Mustang out there. The mere thought filled Peck with rage. His car was his most prized possession. It was, strangely, also his most hated possession. His father had always loved cars. He loved talking about cars. He loved reading about cars. He loved dragging his son to car show after car show to stare helplessly at cars the man could never own. It was pathetic.

And of all the cars his father loved, he loved the Skyway Mustang most of all. So, the minute Peck could afford it, he ran out and bought one just to spite the memory of his dad. To show him just how pathetic he'd been. It was the happiest day of Alton Peck's life. To own another man's favorite thing, just because he could, and they couldn't? What was better than that?

"Ursula, honey," Alton Peck said. He wasn't talking to his desktop Ursula, because he'd smashed that one to bits shortly after realizing it had synced up with the accountant's. No, Peck was talking to the Mother Ursula herself; the massive super-computer and AI brain of Pangea.

"Yes, Mr. Peck," the Mother Ursula answered as a holographic digital face suddenly appeared in the middle of the room.

"Find me all the registered 1964 Mustangs in the Chicago area."

"Yes, sir." In a moment the Mother Ursula scanned all the DMV databases within three counties to find forty-seven 1964 Mustangs in the greater Chicagoland area. Eighteen of them were black. Three of those were convertibles. Alton Peck then ordered the Mother Ursula to run the VIN numbers on the three black 1964 Mustangs. One was a Skyway.

"I have a VIN match, sir," the Ursula said. "A Mr. Derrick Louis Edmonds in Evanston, Illinois, owns a Raven Black 1964 World's Fair Skyway Mustang."

Alton Peck was furious. The gall, the audacity. Someone else in Chicago had his car. Someone else was driving around his city in a Raven Black 1964 World's Fair Skyway Mustang. This Derrick Edmonds was practically mocking him. Well, not for long.

"Find it," Alton Peck said to the Mother Ursula. "Find that car. Now."

Sore. Winner.

Parker found Oona in the impound lot, sitting on the hood of a Chevy Nova and staring intently into Charley's phone.

"Whatcha doing?" Parker said.

"Not much."

"You know, I kind of expected to find you out here narrating."

Oona put the phone back in her pocket. "I decided to take a break from that for a while."

"Aw, really? I thought it was cool."

Oona sighed. "I did, too. But lately, I don't know. The problem with talking to yourself all the time is that no one else can ever get a word in. You think you're arguing with Mr. Mathis, or your parents, or Wade." She laughed a little. "But you're really just fighting with yourself. Because after a while, all you hear is you, and that's not good. I mean, when I first started narrating into my phone, it was supposed to be a way to collect my thoughts and ideas. To find my voice. But lately it's become more like . . ."

"A place to hide?"

"Yeah." Oona nodded. "Exactly."

"I get that. I feel the same way about those videos I make.

They're fun. And some of them are even pretty good. But they're safe. I'm not putting anything of myself out there. I'm just goofing off what somebody else already did."

Oona said, "Maybe you're trying to find your voice, too."

Parker laughed. "Yeah, maybe I am." They were quiet for a minute. "You know, we could try together. Find our voices, I mean."

"You mean, like, collaborate?"

"Why not? We would be an unstoppable comic duo. The next Key and Peele. What do you say?"

Oona said, "I'd like that."

"Charleston Chews," Jed grumbled as the brothers scanned the snack aisle.

"What?"

"Charleston Chews," Jed repeated. "They don't have any."

"So get a PayDay," Ned said.

"I did."

"And it's Charleston *Chew*," Ned said. "No *s*."

"Whatever," Jed growled.

"It is," Ned insisted. "Look on the label."

"I can't, idiot. Because they didn't have any."

The brothers paid and left the convenience store. After they'd missed the accountant at the arcade, AP had rung Ned, called them morons, and said the tracker was now going north again on I-94. Ned and Jed got back in the car and followed, but then the signal disappeared completely at a convenience store in Rogers Park.

Since they'd hit a dead end, the brothers decided to go inside for some caffeine and candy while they waited for AP to call them back, call them morons some more, and tell them what to do next.

Ned stared vacantly at the impound lot across the street when his brother's cell phone rang.

"Yeah." Jed picked it up immediately. "What you got, AP?"

"Put me on speaker," Alton Peck snapped.

Jed did as he was told and put the phone on the dash.

"All right, Moron One and Moron Two. Listen carefully. Ned, check your phone."

Ned did. There was a new app on the home screen labeled OPEN IT, STUPID. He tapped the app, which opened a GPS map with a little blue dot heading north on I-94.

"The tracker's back up?" Jed said enthusiastically, his mouth full of PayDay.

"Obviously. Now get moving."

Jed whipped out of the parking lot while Ned monitored the little blue dot on his phone. The little blue dot that he hadn't asked for, from the app that just appeared on his phone (and insulted him, no less) because someone else decided it should be there. What did it even do, besides obviously tracking the other Mustang up the interstate? Was it tracking them, too? Listening to them? Watching them?

"We've got them now," Jed said excitedly as he gunned it toward the on-ramp. "Technology, huh? Pretty nice."

Ned wasn't so sure.

They were about twenty minutes shy of the Wisconsin border when Wade finally piped up, "So, um, any idea when you'd like to get rid of this thing?"

"Just a little farther," Greg said.

Then Charley said, "Greg, pull over at that next exit."

"What? Why?"

Charley pointed at a gas station visible from the interstate. Where a massive Pangea delivery truck was filling up.

"Ooh," Wade chuckled. "Perfect."

"They stopped at a gas station in Gurnee, just off the interstate," Ned said, staring intently at the little blue dot on his phone.

Jed hit the gas hard, and he'd already been doing eighty. "We've got 'em now," he muttered to himself.

Meanwhile, back in his office, Alton Peck was also watching the little dot, which the Mother Ursula projected as a holographic, three-dimensional grid map.

At the same time, it scoured all the live traffic cam footage in a sixty-mile radius, hunting for Derrick Edmonds's Mustang.

"Target acquired," the Mother Ursula announced.

"Are you sure it's the right one?"

"Make, model, and license plate confirmed," the Mother Ursula said. "This is the car belonging to Mr. Derrick Edmonds."

"Show me."

The Mother Ursula projected video of a convertible 1964 Raven Black World's Fair Skyway Mustang crossing an intersection and pulling into the same gas station where the little blue dot had currently stopped.

"So, the tracker is in that Mustang?"

"That is correct."

"Replay video. Enlarge and enhance."

Ursula replayed the video so that Peck could see who was in

the car. A teenage boy with a kid, a girl, in the passenger seat. And another kid, a boy, in the back.

Peck was confused but only for a moment. While he was waiting for Ursula to locate the other Skyway Mustang, he also had her access all of Derrick Edmonds's social media accounts. Which led to the social media accounts of a woman named Tamara Jeanine Decker. *Her* social media accounts prominently featured her two kids, Gregory and Charlene (eighteen and twelve, respectively). The same kids Peck was looking at now.

He added up the facts. Two kids go for a joyride in their mom's boyfriend's car, stop for a bite at New Farouk's, and wind up with a drugged accountant in their trunk. It was positively ridiculous, but at the same time, it made sense.

Well, this joyride was just about over.

Charley, Wade, and Greg watched as the Pangea driver topped off his tank and went inside the convenience mart to pay for the gas and get some snacks for the road.

"Okay," Charley said. "Now."

Wade jumped out of the car with a roll of duct tape in one hand and Mitch's live ID tag in the other. He went over to the blind side of the truck and taped the tag to the underside of the back bumper, then hightailed it back to the car.

"Anyone see me?"

"Nope," Greg said. "You made it free and clear. Now we just watch and wait."

The driver came back to his truck, got in, and drove off. From their vantage point, they could see the truck get back on the highway, heading north.

"With any luck, they'll follow that truck all the way to Canada."

Alton Peck watched as the blue dot left the gas station and headed north again on I-94. Something didn't feel right.

Then the Mother Ursula said, "Incongruity."

"What do you mean?"

"Incongruity is the state of being incompatible or out of place—"

"I know what the word means! Why are you saying it?"

"Traffic camera footage does not show a convertible 1964 Raven Black World's Fair Skyway Mustang leaving the gas station."

"What does it show?"

The Mother Ursula displayed footage of a Pangea delivery truck passing a four-way traffic light on the way back to the interstate.

Those kids had dumped the tracker. Clever. And it had almost worked.

"Ursula," he said. "Get me the morons."

THIRTEEN

6:04 A.M.

It's possible for a good idea to be a mistake at the same time. For example, Greg's idea to use the tracker to lead the Woznikowski brothers away from the others was smart. And if Alton Peck hadn't been able to hack into all the traffic cameras in Northern Illinois, it would have worked.

After the Pangea truck left, Greg pulled the Mustang around to the back of the gas station, behind the main building. He planned to sit tight for a while so the truck could put some distance between them before he and Charley and Wade headed back to Chicago.

This was another example of a good idea also being a mistake. Because while they were waiting, Peck had warned the Woznikowski brothers not to follow the Pangea truck and instead to go directly to the gas station. And hanging around gave the goons a chance to catch up to them.

"All right," Greg said. "I think that's long enough."

"Finally," Wade sighed in relief. "Let's get out of here."

"I'll text Oona and let her know we're on our way," Charley added.

Greg was just about to start up the car when they heard a *tap-tap-tap* on the driver's side window. It was Jed Woznikowski, revolver in hand. On the passenger side was Ned Woznikowski. He had a gun, too, only he wasn't tapping on the window with it.

"All right, guys," Ned said through the glass. "You gave it a good run, but the game's over."

Ned loaded Charley, Wade, and Greg into the back seat of the twins' Monte Carlo and started driving back to Pangea. Jed followed in the Mustang. Their boss was very explicit about wanting the car brought to him as well.

"Word of advice, kids," Ned warned. "When we get to headquarters, just tell AP whatever he wants to know. It'll all go a lot easier on you. Trust me."

"You put an accountant in the trunk of my car," Greg scoffed. "Why in the world should we trust you?"

"You know," Charley said quietly to Wade, "this would be the perfect time to bust out that 'I told you so' you've been saving all night."

Wade shook his head. "Nah. Not yet."

They drove in silence for a long while as Charley tried to convince herself things weren't as bad as they seemed. Sure she was scared, but it was a kind of faraway scared. Like she knew at some point in the very near future she'd be full-on terrified, but that moment was still a little ways off.

"So," Greg said to her. "What did you do to get detention?"

"What?"

"Your school called the house. You know, those automated messages they send parents if your kid is absent or tardy . . . or gets detention."

Crud. She'd forgotten all about those.

"I mouthed off to Mr. Bonino."

"I thought you liked him."

"I do," Charley admitted. "It wasn't really about him."

Wade, meanwhile, was looking out the window. A few lanes over, a white Escalade was driving erratically. Music blared from the car, even with all the windows up. The guys inside were a bunch of cheesy poser types.

Total aggro-bros.

"Hey," Wade whispered to Charley. "I kind of have an idea. It's stupid, but . . ."

"I'll take stupid right now," Charley said.

Wade looked back out the window. He kept staring at the white Escalade until someone inside noticed him. And then he started making kissy faces.

As he'd hoped, the jerks in the white Escalade totally overreacted to a kid making fun of them. Within seconds the Escalade crossed two lanes to cut in front of the Woznikowskis' Monte Carlo. Ned had to slam on the breaks to avoid a collision.

"What the what?!" he mumbled as the Escalade continued to harass the Monte Carlo. Cutting it off, pulling alongside it, trying to force it into the shoulder of the interstate.

Ned's phone rang.

"I don't know!" he yelled into the phone. "They just started messing with me!" Ned listened and then said, "What do you want to do?"

Ned listened and then abruptly pulled over to the shoulder. The Escalade pulled over in front of him, and the four guys inside got out, looking to bring some pain.

"You got to be kidding me," said Charley.

"Wait," Greg said, catching on. "Are those the aggro-bros from the convenience store?"

"And the arcade," Charley said. She couldn't believe it. But there they were, Puka (aka Dirk, aka Dirk the Jerk) and his entire crew. Again.

Puka (aka Dirk, aka Dirk the Jerk) and his pals surrounded the Monte Carlo, shouting and banging on the hood and windows.

What they hadn't yet noticed was the Mustang pulling in behind the Monte Carlo.

Wade, Charley, and Greg shared a look. With luck, while the Woznikowskis were brawling it out on the side of the road, they would have a chance to make a break for it.

Only it didn't happen that way at all.

For starters, Ned didn't even move. He just sat there and watched them pound on his car with a bored, slightly per-turbed look. Meanwhile, Jed was already out of the Mustang and heading toward the foursome.

What happened next took less than a minute. The four guys charged Jed, who put them all on the ground in about ten seconds. It wasn't what Charley and the others had hoped for, but they had to admit, it was kind of amazing. Jed Woznikowski was like a one-man bar fight. He made demolishing those guys look easy. A punch here, a body toss there, a headbutt to mix things up. Even when one of the guys did manage to land a fist on Jed, he just shrugged it off without a second thought.

Once all the convenience store aggro-bros were on the pavement, cradling the body parts that had received the most abuse, Jed looked back at the Monte Carlo and motioned for his brother to pop the trunk.

And then he got out a baseball bat.

For the next twenty to twenty-five seconds, Jed Woznikowski proceeded to pulverize the Escalade. Windshield, headlights, windows, hood—he pounded all of it until the luxury SUV was a creaking, groaning hunk of metal. Then he calmly tossed the bat in the trunk of the Monte Carlo on his way back to the Mustang.

"Well," Wade sighed. "I got nothing."

A good idea can be a mistake, but sometimes a bad idea can be accidentally brilliant. Wade's idea to goad Puka (aka Dirk, aka Dirk the Jerk) and the convenience store crew into running Ned Woznikowski off the interstate was not smart. It was reckless, not to mention extremely dangerous. And it had a very slim margin for success.

But it wasn't, ultimately, a mistake. Because back at the

impound lot, Oona was still tracking Wade's phone. So when Ned Woznikowski pulled to the shoulder of the interstate, Oona immediately texted Wade to see what had gone wrong. When Wade didn't answer because his phone, along with Greg's, had been confiscated and thrown in the glove compartment, she got worried.

"What if the Woznikowskis got them?" Marisa said anxiously.

"They'll probably take them somewhere to interrogate them," Mitch said. "About my Ursula."

"Where?"

"How would I know?"

"I could scan all the files from Alton Peck's Ursula for clues," Michaela suggested.

"Okay," Oona said desperately. "Try that."

"That'll take forever," Mitch said.

"Well," Marisa snapped. "If you have any other way of figuring out where the Woznikowskis might be taking my boyfriend, I'd love to hear it!"

"You know," Parker said, thoughtfully. "Maybe we could just ask them."

Five minutes later, Michaela was searching the files from Alton Peck's Ursula.

"Okay," she said. "What are we looking for?"

"Any information associated with the name Woznikowski," Marisa said.

Michaela searched. "Nope. No Woznikowskis in his contacts."

Marisa deflated. "Shoot."

"Hold on," Oona said. "Try checking his recent phone activity."

"Okay," Michaela said. "Ah. Here it is."

"What?"

"He's made several calls to someone listed as 'Moron One.' And there's a 'Moron Two' as well."

"Must be them. The Woznikowskis."

"Have you heard from Oscar?" Marisa asked Oona.

"His mom's plane just landed at O'Hare. The FBI team is meeting her on the tarmac. Should be here in about half an hour."

"It's gonna be close," Marisa fretted. "You think Parker can really pull this off?"

"I hope so," Oona said. "Because I don't even want to think about what is going to happen if he doesn't."

"I'm just not getting it," Parker sighed. "I mean, I can do the voice. But I'm not feeling the *character*, you know?"

While the girls searched the hard drive, Parker and Mitch had gone outside so Parker could research and perfect his Alton Peck impersonation. So far he'd watched a couple of interviews and a few minutes of a TED talk, but he was hitting a wall. Something was missing.

"It's because that's not who he really is," Mitch said, indicating the videos on Parker's phone. "He can really turn on the charm when he wants to, but in real life he's a total jerk. I mean, he straight-up goes out of his way to be as cruel as possible. It's kind of sad, actually."

"Huh," Parker said.

"Here, take a look at this." Mitch handed Parker his phone.

"What is it?"

"Pangea corporate retreat two years ago," Mitch explained. "Someone snuck in their cell phone and recorded him."

Parker watched the video on Mitch's phone. Alton Peck was out in the woods, berating two dozen employees in front of a ropes course.

"Is this supposed to be a team-building exercise?"

"Uh-huh."

"Man, he really is a jerk," Parker marveled. "Thanks, Mitch. This is perfect."

"So, what did you say?" Greg asked.

"What?"

"To Mr. Bonino. Why'd he give you detention?"

Charley knew her brother well enough to know he was acting like he wasn't scared to distract *her* from being scared. It wasn't working. But she also knew he wasn't going to let the matter drop. He'd keep pestering her until she told him, mortal danger or not.

Charley sighed. "This girl in my history class tried to get me in trouble by saying I used a curse word in class."

"Did it work?"

"If it did," Charley said, getting snippy, "I wouldn't have said *tried*, would I?"

"Then how did you wind up with detention?"

Charley scratched her head. "Well, I explained to Mr. Bonino that the word I used wasn't a curse word. So then he chalked it up to a misunderstanding. But I said it *wasn't* a misunderstanding— the girl was wrong and an ignorant tattletale and . . ."

Charley trailed off, hoping she could leave it there.

"And . . ." Greg prodded.

"And . . . I *may* have told Mr. Bonino that while it was his job to be patient with ignorant tattletales, it wasn't mine. Or something like that."

Greg laughed. "And that's when you got detention?"

"Yep."

Greg sat there thinking for a few moments. Then he snapped his fingers and said, *"Fluckadrift."*

"What?"

"That was the word you said. The curse word that isn't a curse word: *fluckadrift.*"

Charley's jaw dropped in shock. "That's right," she managed.

"It means, hold on . . ." he started, racking his brain. "Oh, yeah. It means urgency or haste. Like to be in a big hurry."

"How did *you* know that?" she said, hoping he didn't take it as patronizingly as it sounded.

"You used it in Scrabble a few weeks ago, remember? Family game night. Double word score. *Luck* was already on the board— that was mine, by the way—and you built off that. Used all your letters. Most baller Scrabble move I've ever seen. I texted Marisa about it from the table. We couldn't believe it."

Charley felt her eyes well up. "Really?" she choked, which

made her frustrated, which, of course, made her choke up more.

"Hey, hey," Greg said soothingly. "Don't worry about it, okay? It was just detention. We don't even have to tell Mom."

Charley laughed a little. Even when he got it, Greg was still pretty clueless. But that's big brothers for you.

In the front seat, Ned Woznikowski answered his cell phone.

"AP?" he said, confused. "What? This is Ned." There was a pause as Ned listened. "What do you mean change of plans?"

FOURTEEN

6:43 A.M.

Before his parents built a sound studio in their basement, Parker's favorite prank calls had been to high-profile targets. He never went for low-hanging fruit. It wasn't much fun calling up some random little old lady, giving her a gag name, and tricking her into accidentally saying something gross. No, if Parker was going to prank somebody, it had to be someone worth the effort, like the school superintendent, or a right-wing radio host, or the Pentagon. And every time, even if he was blowing it, Parker was always as cool as a cucumber.

This time was different. This time he was pranking two kidnappers who had captured his friends. This time he was more than nervous—he was scared. He couldn't afford to screw up; this time it really mattered.

"Ready?" Oona asked Michaela, who sat with Parker at the desk in front of her computer.

"Ready," she said.

"What about you?" Marisa asked Parker.

He just nodded. Michaela put the call through on her computer while Parker licked his lips and repositioned the microphone.

"AP?" said a voice that was clearly coming from inside a moving car.

"Yeah," Parker began rather shakily. "I mean, yes. This is AP. Um, which one is this?"

"What?" There was an awkward pause on the other end. Then, finally: "This is Ned."

"Okay, Ned. Listen, we've got a change of plans."

"What do you mean change of plans?"

"I want you guys to come straight to this address," he said as Michaela scribbled down the address for the impound lot on a scrap of paper.

"Wait. You don't want us to bring the kids and the Mustang to Pangea anymore?"

"No," Parker said carefully. "Too much exposure. The place I'm talking about is an impound lot. It's quiet, isolated. Follow me?"

There was another long pause. Something wasn't working. Though Parker's impression of Alton Peck was technically spot-on, he didn't *sound* like the tech villain. Not really. Parker knew it, too. A bead of sweat snaked down the side of his head.

Mitch pointed at the paper Michaela had scribbled on. "Can I use this?" he mouthed soundlessly.

Michaela handed him the paper. Mitch flipped it over; he quickly wrote something down and handed it to Parker.

Parker read the note.

Find the character—BE THE JERK!

It was just the directorial note Parker needed.

"Did I stutter!" Parker barked into the microphone.

"What? No. No, AP."

"Then am I going too fast for you? Should I have called the other moron instead and told him what to do?"

"I got it, boss. Really. I got it."

"Repeat the address back to me so I know," Parker said, getting into it now.

Ned repeated the address.

"Hey, look at that! First try and everything. Maybe you're not such a moron after all. I'll be sure to alert the folks at Mensa. Tell them to look out for you."

"Huh?"

Oona and Mitch motioned frantically for Parker to wrap it up.

"Never mind," Parker said hurriedly. "I'll meet you at the impound lot. Just get there as fast as you can. And, um, drive safely."

Parker motioned for Michaela to end the call.

"Drive safely?" Michaela chuckled.

Parker shrugged helplessly.

"Think it worked?" Oona said.

"Oh, he bought it," Marisa said, with relief. "Great job, Parker."

Parker beamed with pride, then looked over at Mitch. "Thanks for the note."

"Glad I could help."

"So, what do we do now?"

"Now we wait. And hope that Senator Zelzah and the Feds get here before the kidnappers do."

Ned Woznikowski was confused. Something about that call with AP had been weird from the jump. Ned couldn't put his finger on it, but AP hadn't sounded right. He'd almost sounded, well, like a human being.

But then, somewhere around the middle of the call, AP had called him a moron and started to sound like himself again. And the more Ned thought about it, going to some out-of-the-way impound lot did make sense, particularly if they were going to rub out these kids.

Ned wasn't sure how he felt about that, though. It was more than just them being kids. What they had done with that accountant's ID tag, putting it on the truck as a decoy, that was clever. It should have worked. It *deserved* to work. Using all the traffic cameras to catch them, though. That felt cheap. It was a garbage move. There needed to be rules, after all. Limits. Some sense of fair play. Even for criminals like him.

One thing still bothered him, though. When AP had called, he'd asked Ned which twin he was. AP never did that. He always treated Ned and Jed like they were interchangeable. He never cared which one of them was which.

Until recently, neither had Ned.

Oona hung up the cell phone. "That was Oscar. His mom is on her way in a helicopter and the FBI guys are going to meet her here."

"When?"

"Twenty minutes. But we'll need a place for her to land."

"We could make room at the back end of the lot," Michaela suggested.

"Perfect."

"We'd have to move some of the cars, though."

Michaela slipped into the office through the back and grabbed a bunch of keys off the board of impounded cars on the back wall.

Michaela's dad, still passed out in the chair behind the counter, didn't even move.

"You weren't kidding," Oona whispered to Michaela. "He really can sleep through anything."

Marisa and Michaela worked out which cars to move and where to create a safe landing zone for Senator Zelzah's helicopter. Then Marisa and Mitch moved the cars to the other end of the lot as quickly as they could. But the last car they needed to move was a Porsche and Marisa kept stalling.

"You're popping the clutch," Michaela said.

"I know, I know, sorry," Marisa groaned. "I suck at stick."

"You could always put it in neutral and we could push," Parker suggested.

"Not helping!" Marisa snapped, but she got it on the next try and scooted the car across the lot. They had their makeshift landing zone.

Now all they had to do was wait.

"Something's changed," Wade said.

Charley noticed it, too. After Ned hung up his cell phone, he quickly got into the right lane on the interstate. His cell phone rang again almost immediately. Though he'd kept his voice low on the last call, he was louder now and they could hear his side of the conversation.

"AP doesn't want us to go to Pangea anymore," Ned said. "Well, how should I know? Some impound lot in Rogers Park. Yeah, he said he's going to meet us there. Just follow me."

Wade looked at Charley and Greg.

Impound lot? he mouthed silently.

This was bad. If they were going to Rogers Park, it could only mean one thing: Peck had found the others. Not only had their decoy plan gotten them captured, it'd also failed to protect everyone else.

Charley started to panic. They had to find some way to warn Oona and the others, but how? The twins had taken their phones.

Ned got off at the next exit. They were only about two miles from the lot now. If they were going to try something, it would have to be soon.

A helicopter flew overhead, going in the same direction. Ned watched it curiously.

Greg gave Charley and Wade a look, then nodded at Wade's door. Charley knew what her brother was going to do. At some point he was going to launch himself into the front seat and try to wrestle control of the car from Ned.

It wouldn't be easy. Greg was on the passenger side. That meant he'd have to lunge all the way across the car. There was no way it would work. Ned would pummel Greg before he even got close to the steering wheel. But in the commotion, Charley and Wade might be able to escape.

In baseball this was called a sacrifice fly.

Charley shook her head vigorously. But there was no fighting it. Greg was her big brother. Her pal, her partner in crime. He always had her back. And there wasn't anything he wouldn't do for her.

Unfortunately, they made all the traffic lights once they got off the exit, and Ned hadn't needed to slow down much. It would be way too dangerous for Charley and Wade to jump out of the car at these speeds.

In no time they were at the impound lot. The gate was open—what did that mean?—and Ned just cruised right in, followed closely by Jed in the Mustang. That helicopter they saw before now hovered directly above them.

When Ned put the car in park and looked up at the helicopter, Greg made his move, desperately lunging over and across the back seat.

"What the—" Ned leaned away as Greg tumbled into the front seat.

Wade grabbed the door handle and was just about to open it when he stopped short.

A hulking man in a black suit was pointing a gun at the car.

Charley looked around and saw that the car was surrounded by several hulking men in black suits. They were all pointing guns and shouting over the sound of the landing helicopter: "Federal agents! Do not move!"

No one moved.

"What in the world—"

Mr. Daftari fell out of his chair as two FBI agents rushed into the office. Until that very moment he'd slept like a baby through a helicopter landing, sirens, screeching cars, slamming doors, and a cacophony of shouting law enforcement personnel. But the minute the agents tripped the shopkeeper's bell on the front door, Michaela's father instantly jolted awake.

"FBI, Mr. Daftari," one of the agents said as the other swept the room. "Please stay where you are, for your own safety."

A few minutes later, the agents led Michaela's groggy father out of the office and into the utter chaos that had completely taken over his place of business. At the front gate, agents were shouting and pointing their guns at a beat-up Monte Carlo. And at the back end of the lot, a helicopter's rotors were slowing to a stop. Poor Mr. Daftari didn't know what to think.

Then he noticed Charley as she got out of the Monte Carlo.

"Oh, you have to be kidding me," Mr. Daftari moaned. "Not you again."

Ned Woznikowski did not resist arrest. When the federal agents told him to get out of the car slowly, he did what he was told.

Jed did resist. Quite a bit. It took three agents to subdue him, and even when they did, he yelled and cursed the whole way into the back of one of the black sedans.

The thing of it was, Ned was kind of glad they'd gotten caught. Not the getting arrested and going to jail part—he wasn't looking forward to any of that. And he couldn't figure out how the kids had pulled it off. He knew that, somehow, he and his brother had been led into a trap, but he didn't know how. If he was being honest with himself, though, he was more impressed than put out about it. Kind of like when you see a really cool magic trick. He was even a little relieved.

He wondered if they'd gotten AP, too. He hoped they had. AP was out of control. There had to be rules. You could only rig the game so much, otherwise things just went to . . . there had to be limits.

The agents put Ned in the back of one of the other black sedans. Jed was still kicking and screaming inside his. He was really mad, and for a moment it made Ned feel kind of guilty that he wasn't really mad, too. But mostly knowing all this craziness was out of his hands felt good. Ned decided that if the Feds asked him questions, he'd answer them. He'd tell them everything they wanted to know about AP.

And for a moron, he knew some things.

FIFTEEN

8:23 A.M.

FBI agent Karen Hill sat up in her chair. "Okay, Charley. Let's try this again from the beginning."

"You're wasting your time," Charley protested, for what felt like the hundredth time. "You need to be out there, finding Alton Peck before he—"

"Excuse me," Agent Hill said, perturbed. "Please don't tell us how to do our jobs."

"Somebody has to," Charley grumbled. That probably wasn't smart. They'd been going back and forth like this for a while now, with no signs of letting up. This Agent Hill was one stubborn woman. Almost as stubborn as Charley.

Charley looked up at the two-way mirror that lined the wall behind Agent Hill. If they weren't listening to her, maybe whoever was behind that mirror would.

"Have you guys even looked at that stuff from Peck's Ursula?" Charley yelled at the mirror. "Do you even get what this guy has done? What he's trying to do?"

"C'mon, kid. Take it easy," Agent Hill's partner pleaded.

A tall woman in a designer suit walked into the room. "All right," she said. "I think that's enough for now."

The two agents straightened up immediately. So did Charley. The woman had that effect on people.

"But Senator Zelzah," Agent Hill protested. "The witness is being evasive and combative."

"The witness is being a seventh grader."

"Yeah," Charley chimed in.

The senator gave her a weary, *why-couldn't-you-just-leave-it-alone* look that made Charley suddenly miss her mom.

After the bust at the impound lot, Charley and Wade and everyone were taken directly downtown to the FBI field office for questioning. That is, everyone except for Michaela, who was still walking half the FBI's cyberterrorism unit through the ins and outs of Mitch's Ursula, and poor Mitch himself, who'd been scooped up by US Marshals and whisked off to protective custody.

Charley had spent the last forty minutes or so explaining the events of the evening to Special Agent Hill and her partner, Special Agent Dale (don't bother, they've heard all the jokes). But at long last, the interview was over. Senator Zelzah ushered her into the hallway, where Charley found Greg and her friends loitering.

"About time," Wade said.

"We were getting worried," Oona added.

Charley gave Greg a puzzled look. "What are they talking about?"

"We've all been waiting for you," Greg explained. "The rest of us have been done for almost twenty minutes."

Charley felt embarrassed. "Even Oona?" she tried desperately.

"Let's see about getting you guys some breakfast," Senator Zelzah said diplomatically.

The senator took them all down to the commissary for some food. They were met there by Oscar. He was flanked by two agents, who stuck by his side all the way to the senator's table, just in case he somehow got turned around in the dining hall.

"Never a dull moment with you guys, is there?" Oscar joked as he bumped fists with Greg and Charley.

While they all sat down to eat, Charley and the others gave Oscar a more detailed account of everything that had happened since they'd dropped him off at the fraternity a few hours and a million years earlier. The dining hall was completely empty and Charley suddenly wondered if that wasn't by design. They were, after all, talking about some highly touchy issues of national security.

"You are going to arrest him, aren't you?" Greg said, drawing the senator into the conversation. "Alton Peck? He's not going to get away with it, right?"

Senator Zelzah shook her head. "He's not going to get away with it," she assured the kids. "In fact, a team of agents should be raiding Pangea headquarters as we speak. I hope to get an update any minute."

Oscar's mom exuded confidence, but Charley detected a sliver of uncertainty behind it. She had caught the senator checking her phone more than once during breakfast, and guessed that they might be overdue for that update.

"Senator?" Marisa ventured a bit warily. "What exactly happens to us now?"

"You go home," the senator said.

"That's it?"

"More or less."

"Just to be clear," Wade said carefully. "We're not in any trouble?"

"Are you kidding? You guys are national heroes."

"Not so sure our parents will see it that way."

Senator Zelzah smiled. "Well, funny you should say that. See, everything that happened in the last fifteen hours is now a matter of national security. Which means, for the time being, you're not allowed to discuss any of it. With anyone."

There was a moment of silence as everyone took in the implications of what she was saying.

Parker snickered. "You mean the US government is officially forbidding us to tell our parents about what went down last night?"

"Correct, Mr. Nadal."

"Dude. That's . . . an unexpectedly welcome turn of events."

The FBI agents had wanted to keep the Mustang as evidence, but fortunately Senator Zelzah talked them out of it.

"We have the accountant; we don't need the car," she said patiently. "Besides, these kids can't very well keep their mouths shut without it."

Oscar and his mom offered to take Parker home on their way back to campus. It was funny how whenever the senator was around her son, Charley just saw her as a mom, and not one of the most powerful members of Congress. She remembered the sight of Senator Zelzah stepping off the helicopter while the FBI agents swarmed the impound lot. It was, without a doubt, a serious way to make an entrance. At the same time, it had to be hard having someone like that as your mom. Kids joked about having helicopter parents, but Oscar's actually had the helicopter.

"Excuse me," Senator Zelzah said suddenly, stepping away to take a call.

Charley watched her carefully. Though she couldn't hear what the senator was saying, she could tell by her subtle change in body language that this was not the information she'd been hoping to get. Senator Zelzah ended her call and rejoined the others.

"I'm afraid I have some bad news," she said directly. "Alton Peck got away."

"But how is that even possible?" Marisa said. "You sent all those agents."

"It turns out he had a secret elevator in his office that took him to a private escape tunnel under the building."

"Whoa!" Parker exclaimed. "How cool is that!"

"Parker!" Oona scolded.

"Well, it is. I mean, look, the dude is straight-up evil. But you got to respect his game."

"He could be anywhere," Charley said.

"We'll find him," Senator Zelzah said confidently. "Peck is now on every watch list you can think of. Plus he's one of the most recognizable people in the world. If he even steps foot in an airport or a train station or a bus depot, we'll be on him in a heartbeat. Not to mention the inspection stops the FBI set up on all the highways out of Illinois. He's got nowhere to go. Trust me, it's just a matter of time."

It was a quiet drive back to Evanston. Nobody said much. Charley tried to sort out her feelings as they dropped Parker off, and it wasn't easy. She was relieved that they were all safe and sound and had the car back. But she was also afraid—Alton Peck was in the wind and there was nothing any of them could do about it. On top of that, she was still pumped from all the excitement and danger. Sure, she was glad the chaos was all over. Still, it had been a rush.

Charley let Wade and Oona into the house, while Greg dropped Marisa off at her car, which was still parked back on campus. Right away Wade plopped down on the couch.

"All right," he said. "Who's up for a movie?"

Charley laughed. She was beyond exhausted, but a part of her was way too wired to even think about sleeping. "What did you have in mind?"

"Hmmm," Wade considered. "*Hot Fuzz*? *Galaxy Quest*?"

"Both solid."

"You know, we should really let Oona pick. Seeing as she saved our lives and all."

"Sure. It's only fair."

Oona wasn't listening; her head was buried in Charley's phone. Now that Charley thought about it, Oona had been on that phone ever since they'd left the field office. At first Charley thought Oona might be narrating again, but she hadn't made a peep the whole car ride back.

"Oona, what do you feel like?"

Oona looked up. She had a confused, troubled look on her face. "Sorry," she said.

"What's up?" Wade asked.

"I'm not sure," Oona said. "It's weird. After breakfast, Senator Zelzah asked me to send her the link to that article I found. The one about Alton Peck getting the Skyway Mustang to honor his dad. Remember?"

"Sure."

"Only I can't find it."

"It should be right there in the search history."

"I know. But it's not. I even tried to google it again. Nothing."

"How can that be?"

"Well, there are still lots of articles about Peck, and a couple do mention his Skyway Mustang. But I can't find that specific article at all. It's like it disappeared."

"He did it," Wade said quietly. "That's what you think, isn't it? You think he scrubbed the article from the internet."

Oona's eyes said it all. That was exactly what she thought.

"But you can't do that, can you?" Charley protested. "I mean, you can't just erase something from the entire internet."

"Apparently," Wade said, "he can."

In a strange way, that frightened Charley more than the Woznikowskis ever did. She willed herself to focus.

"Why that article?" she wondered aloud.

"What?"

"You said that it was the only article about Alton Peck you couldn't find. Why that one?"

Wade caught on first. "There's something in that article, some information he wants to hide."

"Like what?" Oona said. "Evidence or something?"

"Maybe," Charley said. "Oona, you read the whole thing, right? How much do you remember?"

Oona shrugged. "I don't know. It was a long article. It talked about Alton Peck's past, where he grew up. How he started Pangea with a small personal loan from his father. Then there was the bit about the Mustang, obviously."

"We already know about the Mustang," Charley reasoned. "There'd be no reason to hide that."

"Hold on," Wade said. "We're thinking about this all wrong. Alton Peck is on the run. All he cares about right now is getting away. Maybe he scrubbed that article because it had some clue about where he's going."

Oona closed her eyes and tried to concentrate. "Um, um . . ."

"Try to picture the article. Focus on places, locations."

"I'm trying!" she snapped. Oona could see vague snippets of the article in her mind, but they were playing hide-and-seek with her memory.

Waiting for him on the tarmac was his prized possession, a convertible Raven Black 1964 World's Fair Skyway Mustang . . .

It was right there, she knew it. Hiding in plain sight.

Waiting for him on the tarmac . . .

on the tarmac . . .

"A tarmac," she said slowly.

"Like an airport?" Charley offered.

Oona shook her head. Not an airport, but . . .

She gritted her teeth, it was so close.

"Not an airport," Oona said. "Smaller."

Charley and Wade, desperate to help, started throwing words at Oona.

"Airfield?"

"Runway?"

"Heliport?"

"Aerodrome?"

"Aerodrome? Seriously?"

"Hey, like heliport was a real winner."

"All right, fair enough."

"Guys," Oona cut in. "This isn't helping."

"Landing strip?"

"That's it!"

"Landing strip?"

"No," Oona said. Not a landing strip. But close.

. . . a private airstrip.

That was it.

Alton Peck's plane landed at the private airstrip . . .

This had to be it. But where? Where was the airstrip?

. . . the private airstrip he built outside his hometown of Fox Lake, Illinois.

"Fox Lake!" Oona exclaimed. "That's where the interview took place. Fox Lake, Illinois! At Alton Peck's private airstrip."

"You think that's why he made the article disappear?" Wade said. "Because it mentions the airstrip?"

"Uh-huh."

"He must have a plane waiting."

"That's where he's going," Charley said. "That's how he's getting away."

"What are you guys going on about?" Greg said as he came in the front door.

"We know where Alton Peck is," Charley said. "He has a private airstrip in Fox Lake. That's how he's going to get out of the country."

Charley and Wade explained to Greg about the article that mysteriously vanished from the internet because it mentioned the airstrip. Oona, meanwhile, was back on Charley's phone.

"Look, I get how the article disappearing is odd," Greg said skeptically. "But you have to admit, it's still a pretty thin lead."

"There's more," Oona said, looking up from the phone. "Or, to put it more accurately, less."

"Oona," Greg sighed. "I'm really tired."

"There's nothing online about an airport, or an airstrip, or even a landing strip anywhere in Fox Lake. Past or present. As far as the internet is concerned, it never existed."

"So now he's made an entire airport disappear, too?"

"Airstrip," Oona corrected as she held out the phone. "You tell me."

The screen showed the Google map for Fox Lake. Off to the

west there was a gray, blank space where the image curiously couldn't load. "Big enough for an airstrip?"

Greg grabbed the phone. "Okay," he said. "I'm convinced."

"Well," Charley said. "Let's go."

"Us?!" Wade said. "To Fox Lake?"

"Wade's right, Charley," Oona said. "We should call this in to the FBI."

"We can do that on the way," Charley protested. "Listen, I'm not saying we try to catch the guy. But it would be enough just to prove the airstrip exists, right? As of now this is still just a hunch."

"Fine," Greg said. "I'll go. You guys stay here."

"No," Wade said. "We all go."

Greg did a double take. He'd expected dissent from his sister, not Wade.

"Dude, by now this guy probably knows everything about us. And he's really good at making things disappear. Splitting up is the worst thing we can do. We need to stick together and keep moving."

"He's right," Oona said. "Besides, if Alton Peck thinks no one knows about the airstrip, he's never going to see us coming. It's the last thing he'd suspect."

Greg drove the Mustang quickly up the interstate.

Charley groaned in frustration as she ended a call on her cell phone.

"They didn't buy it?" Oona said.

"Agent Hill said she'd be sure to pass the tip along," Charley said. "I wouldn't hold your breath."

"Call Oscar?" Wade suggested. "See if he can get his mom to listen?"

It was worth a shot. Unfortunately, Oscar couldn't help, either.

"She won't go for it, Charley," Oscar said. "I know my mom. Besides, she's flying back to DC right now for an emergency meeting with the Senate Intelligence Committee."

"Couldn't you ask her to tell the FBI to check it out?"

"I could, but it wouldn't work. The Feds are already stretched thin looking for Alton Peck. There's no way they'd risk pulling agents off their own leads to investigate an airport that might not even be there."

"Airstrip. And we're on our way there now," Oona protested. They had Oscar on speaker.

"Where?"

"To Fox Lake! To the airstrip!"

"We're going to see for ourselves," Charley said. "If it really is there, would that be enough?"

There was a long pause on the line. "Maybe," Oscar said. "If I saw it myself, I know she'd listen then. Can you come get me?"

Charley looked at Greg, who shook his head. "We're past Evanston," Greg said into the phone. "If we come back for you, we'll lose too much time."

There was a dejected lull in the conversation.

"Hey, wait a minute," Wade said. "Oscar, can you get a car?"

"I suppose. I mean, yeah. One of my fraternity brothers would lend me his. Sure."

Charley picked up the phone. "Oscar, hold on a minute." She put the phone on mute.

"Wade, what are you doing?"

"You heard him, Charley. If he calls his mom from Alton Peck's private airstrip, she'll turn that plane around on a dime."

The helicopter parent with her own helicopter, Charley thought. Wade was right; it was the only way to get the senator to listen.

"Wade," Oona began delicately. "You do realize what you're saying? You're expecting a guy who has absolutely no sense of direction to drive forty-five miles to a remote town to find a private airstrip that, as of one hour ago, isn't even on the map?"

Wade said, "I think he can do it."

"Wade . . ."

"No, hear me out," Wade plowed forward. "I think Oscar's direction problem is mostly about confidence. I mean, you've seen how protective his mom is with him. That's bound to make a guy feel like he can't take care of himself."

"He's treated like he's helpless, so he sees himself as helpless?"

"Kind of. Yeah. But if somebody believes in him, I think he'll rise to the occasion."

"And you think that somebody is us?" Oona asked.

"Well, you," Wade said.

"Me?"

"You're going to talk him through it. No maps, no GPS. Just you on the phone, telling him where to go. Step by step."

"I can't do that."

"Of course you can. It combines two of your greatest strengths: looking out for people and talking."

Oona shook her head vigorously. "It'll never work."

"I'll help," Wade insisted. "We can do this, Oona. Trust me."

Charley looked at Oona and Wade. "Okay?"

Oona bit her lower lip, then said, "Okay."

Charley took the phone off mute. "Oscar, listen up. This is what we're going to do . . ."

SIXTEEN

9:44 A.M.

"Hey," Oscar giggled over the phone. "The compass on the dashboard says *N*. That's for north, right? And that's good because I'm on I-94 North and that's how I'm supposed to be going."

"That's right, Oscar," Oona laughed.

"This isn't hard at all!"

Wade gave Oona a *told-you-so* look, making her blush. Admittedly, it had all gotten off to a rocky start. It'd taken a good five minutes to navigate Oscar out of the parking lot, but then, once Oscar had driven off campus toward the interstate, the three of them had slowly fallen into a rhythm. Though they couldn't track Oscar, per se, Wade was following along with the maps app on his phone as Oona told Oscar what to look for and where to go.

As Wade had expected, Oona was the perfect person for the job. She was supportive without coddling, and her knack for narration sure came in handy.

Wade had been right about Oscar as well. With every successful turn, every intersection navigated, his confidence had grown. By the time he'd gotten on the interstate, he was almost cocky.

"It looks like 134 hits US-12 coming up," Oscar said breezily. "I want to take that north, yes?"

"Yep," Oona said. "You'll take a right at the intersection."

"Got it."

He was about fifteen minutes behind them. Greg was already in Fox Lake, and in the general area of the airstrip, but finding it was a little tricky. There was a lot of blank space on the Google map to drive through.

"There!" Charley said, pointing to a small, paved access road hemmed in with cornfields on either side.

Greg stopped. "What?"

"An antenna," Charley said. "Could be a control tower?"

Greg turned quickly and drove a couple hundred yards through the cornfields until they came to a clearing. It wasn't much. Two thin runways, with an office building in front and a hangar on either side. Easy to miss. Easy to disappear.

"This is it."

Greg pulled into the gravel lot and parked in front of the main building. It was small, single-story, sleek, and modern but in a blending-into-the-background kind of way.

They all got out of the car to take a closer look. The front doors were locked.

"Stay here," Greg said as he jogged to the other end of the building, toward the far hangar.

Oona got a text on Charley's phone. "I have to go," she said.

"What?"

"That was Oscar. He's about five minutes out. I need to double back to the mouth of this access road," Oona said.

Wade shook his head. "I don't know, Oona."

"I have to," Oona insisted. "He'll drive right past it if someone isn't out there to flag him down."

Charley didn't like the idea of them splitting up. But they had been lucky to spot this road the first time. Oscar would never find it on his own.

"I'll be fine," Oona said. "If there's any trouble, I can just hide in the corn."

They watched as Oona jogged down the road until she disappeared around a bend. Then Wade turned back to look at the building. "Hey, Charley," he said. "Look."

There was a faint light coming from one of the windows.

They went to investigate. Through the window they could see the light was coming from a desk lamp. Next to the desk was an open safe.

"Looks like it's been cleaned out."

"Alton Peck was here."

A voice behind them said, "He still is."

For the briefest of seconds, Charley tried to convince herself that Parker was punking them. But as she and Wade turned around, there was Alton Peck with a gun in his hand. And it was pointed at them.

"Let's go," Peck said coldly, leading them into the first hangar, where his private jet was waiting.

"Hey, you know, I'm really not big on flying," Charley said, stalling for time.

Wade chimed in, "Yeah, I left my Dramamine back—"

"Get on the plane," Alton Peck growled, cocking the gun. "Now."

It was pretty nice as far as private jets go. The cabin was like a mini version of a millionaire's living room. Peck pointed to two cushy, leather seats near the door. "Have a seat," he said.

The pilot came out of the cockpit. "All right, Mr. Peck. Systems check is complete, we— Whoa!"

"Fine," Peck said.

"Sir, you didn't say anything about kids."

Peck pointed his gun at the pilot. "Will that be a problem?"

The pilot looked at the kids, then at the gun, and quickly redrew his moral line in the sand. "Not really," he said.

In the seat across from them, Wade noticed a large duffel bag with the initials *AP* engraved across the front.

As the pilot returned to the cockpit, Peck looked out the windows. "I suppose that brother of yours is around here somewhere."

Wade leaned forward and subtly reached for the duffel bag.

"He went to get help."

"Sure, he did. Not that it matters, either way. We'll be in the air in a few minutes." Peck turned his attention back to the kids and Wade quickly sat back in his seat.

Peck glared at Wade suspiciously. "What were you doing?"

"Nothing. I thought I was going to get airsick, so I was looking for a barf bag."

"We aren't even taxiing yet."

Wade shrugged. But Peck wasn't buying it.

"So, what's your plan?" Charley interjected.

"Well," Peck said casually. "Once we're airborne, I plan to drop you two brats into Lake Michigan. I'm really looking forward to that, I don't mind telling you."

"You know," Wade said. "Killing your hostages kind of defeats the purpose of having hostages."

Alton Peck laughed. "You're not my hostages. I'm just getting rid of you for fun. As revenge for ruining my genius Ursula program. No, I have a much better hostage."

Wade looked around the plane. "Where are they? Because unless this plane has an upstairs, I don't see anyone else."

"Oh, it's not a person," Peck scoffed. "It's something much more important."

Charley got there before Wade.

"The internet," Charley said. "That's your hostage."

Peck looked almost impressed. "That's right," he said.

Of course. This guy managed to make an airstrip virtually disappear in no time at all. What would he make disappear next?

The answer was anything he wanted.

It could work. If he got away, got out of the country, to some island lair he probably owned off the coast of Florida or wherever, he could use those satellites of his to cause all sorts of chaos. Erase economies, rewrite histories, or just put everybody's private personal information out there for everyone else to see.

He could, literally, dox the world.

Wade looked at Charley. "He can't really do that? Hold the internet hostage?"

Charley desperately wanted to say he couldn't. But it probably wouldn't even be that hard. Pretty much everyone in the world either owned a Pangea product, or owned a product with a Pangea processor or microchip or some other component inside it. Alton Peck, like the internet, was everywhere.

How do you defeat a bad guy like that? How do you even try? You might as well punch smoke.

The pilot poked his head out of the cockpit. "Ready to go, sir."

"Excellent," Peck said. "Let's get this show on the road, shall we?"

The first thing Greg saw when he stepped into the other hangar was a yacht. It was white with gold stripes along the bow. Across the transom was the boat's name:

THE BIG WINNER

It took up the entire far wall of the hangar, but it wasn't alone. There were two sailboats next to it. Greg slowly walked deeper into the hangar; it was like the mega-rich version of someone's cluttered garage. There was a Ferrari, a Maserati, a Rolls-Royce, and about a dozen motorcycles. Not to mention statues and sculptures and wooden boxes of art just stacked up against the wall. It should have been impressive, like finding pirate treasure, but Greg actually thought it was really sad. There was a fortune in this hangar, but it was all packed up as if it had no value.

Alton Peck probably didn't even know he had half this stuff. But maybe that wasn't the point. If he had it, then you didn't. For some people, that's what it means to be happy, to be a winner.

Greg turned to leave the hangar. And that's when he saw it. The car was covered, parked off by itself in the farthest corner of the hangar like it was in time-out or something. Greg walked over to it, but he didn't need to take off the canvas to see what was underneath.

He already knew.

Greg heard the sound of a plane engine warming up. He ran to the hangar doors, cracking them open enough to look out on the runway. The nose of a jet plane slowly peeked out from the other hangar.

Alton Peck was getting away!

But it was worse than that. Through the plane's windows he could see that Peck was not alone.

He had Charley and Wade with him.

As the plane slowly taxied onto the runway, Wade looked at Charley.

"Okay," he said. *"Now* I'm going to say I told you so."

Charley choked out a laugh, then reached out her hand. Wade took it.

The plane stopped as the engines revved up the way they do right before takeoff. Alton Peck paced angrily up and down the small cabin, looking out the windows on both sides.

Wade nudged Charley and nodded his head toward a wet bar at the back of the plane. It was stocked with fancy crystal decanters.

"I'm going to make a move for the gun," he said quietly. "When I do, grab one of those bottles and hit him on the head?"

"That's your plan?!"

"It's not a plan," Wade scoffed. "This is desperation."

"It won't work."

"Probably not. But the cabin is pressurized now, so if he's smart, he'll hesitate before shooting that gun."

Charley wasn't so sure about that. Alton Peck was probably one of the smartest people in the world, but he was also one of the angriest. And right now, the anger seemed to be calling the shots.

"Besides," Wade added, "I think I'd rather be shot than thrown out of a plane."

"Okay," Charley said. "Let's do it."

"When he comes back this way, I'll go for him. Then you run for the bar. Got it?"

"Got it."

Peck turned at the front of the cabin and started back their way. Wade scooted forward to the front of his seat and prepared to attack.

"Boss!" the pilot called suddenly from the cockpit.

Peck stopped short. "What?"

"You need to see this."

Peck rushed to the cockpit. "No!" he bellowed, dropping down into the copilot seat. "NO, NO, NO!!!"

Charley and Wade crept forward to see what he was yelling at.

Even before she saw a growing dark flash through the windshield, Charley had a pretty good guess.

Racing down the runway, heading right toward them, was a convertible Raven Black 1964 World's Fair Skyway Mustang. And behind the wheel was her brother. The car came at them like a bullet. Greg shifted seamlessly through the gears, unleashing more power, more speed, more fury as man and machine drove dead at the plane for all they were both worth.

Alton Peck stared out the windshield with the white-hot rage of a thousand bad-guy origin stories. With a homicidal whisper he said: "I hate that car."

"What does he even think he's doing?" the pilot said, pointing out the windshield at the fast-approaching Mustang. "There's no way—"

"Run it down," Peck ordered.

"What?" the pilot said. "You can't be serious."

Peck *was* serious. He was also completely unhinged. Charley was not a licensed psychiatrist, but she could tell that something had been triggered inside Alton Peck. The man had snapped.

"Do it," Peck hissed. "Speed up. Take it out."

"Sir," the pilot protested desperately. "We don't need to play chicken here. I can reach the connector to the second runway before the car will even get close. We can just go around him."

"I'm not playing chicken," Peck cackled maniacally. "I'm going to squash that car like a bug! I'm going to grind it under my heel and pulverize it."

"But we'll crash!"

Peck pointed his gun at the pilot's head. "I SAID RUN IT DOWN!!"

The pilot froze. The Mustang was gaining speed. And though

Charley could barely see inside the car, she was sure she could glimpse her brother through the windshield.

With his shortstop smile.

Alton Peck let out a war cry and reached across the pilot, grabbing the control wheel and shoving the throttle levers forward.

"I'LL SHOW YOU!!!" he screamed.

The last thing Charley saw through the window was the Mustang spinning out in front of the plane seconds before impact. That's when Wade grabbed Charley and pulled her to the relative safety of the back of the plane. When they hit the car, the front section buckled and Wade covered Charley's body with his own, absorbing the impact as they banged against the floor, the ceiling, the seats, walls, and pretty much the entire interior of the main cabin.

And then everything was still.

Charley and Wade lay facedown on the floor of the plane. They heard groaning from the cockpit.

"Oh, shut up," Alton Peck growled at the injured pilot. There was some rustling then as they heard him crawl his way out of the cockpit.

Charley started to stir, but Wade grabbed her arm.

"Don't move," he said in a faint whisper.

They heard Peck cursing and rummaging around the main cabin, then the exit door opening.

"Sounds like he's gone," Wade said a few moments later. "You okay?"

"I think so. You?"

"Yeah."

As they started to get up, a frantic Greg rushed into the cabin.

"Charley! Wade!"

Charley ran to him. "Greg!" she sobbed, burying her head into her brother's chest as she collided into him. The last thing she'd seen was the plane bearing down on the Mustang with Greg inside, and even though she was overjoyed that he was okay, she still didn't understand how it was possible. "I thought . . . I thought . . ."

"Hey," Greg said soothingly as she cried. "I'm fine, Charley. Really. How are you guys?"

"All right," Wade said, looking around the cabin.

"Let's get out of here."

"In a minute," Wade said, still looking.

"What?" Charley said, wiping her eyes.

"It's gone. The duffel bag. Peck took it with him."

If Charley hadn't been so overwhelmed with relief that they were all still alive, she might have noticed that Wade didn't sound like that was a bad thing.

"Never mind," Greg said, and led them carefully out of the wreckage of the plane.

Out in the light of morning, Charley and Wade could see road rash on Greg's face and down his arms.

"Aw, man," Wade said, impressed. "You dove free while the car was spinning out, didn't you?"

Greg nodded. "Coolest thing I'll ever do, and no one was even there to see it," he quipped.

Another groan came from the cockpit.

"He saw it," Charley said, pointing to the pilot, who was still trapped in his seat in the crumpled nose of the plane, which rested like a boulder on the flattened remains of the Mustang.

"Oh no," Wade said, tearing up a little himself now. He put a tender hand on the wreckage of the car. "It's just not fair."

Charley's stomach dropped. "What are we going to tell Derrick?"

Greg shrugged. "Why should we tell him anything? It's not his car."

As Greg explained about Alton Peck's hangar full of trophies and how he found the identical Mustang that started this whole fiasco in the first place, Charley spotted a car turning onto the runway.

Oscar screeched to a stop at the plane, and Oona hopped out of the car, running straight for her friends. Oscar lagged behind, talking on his cell phone.

"No, Ma. It's forty-two degrees, twenty-four minutes, and twelve seconds north *latitude*. Right. And eighty-eight degrees, eleven minutes, and thirty-one seconds west longitude. Uh-huh. Ma, I don't care what the FBI guys are telling you. I'm standing right in the middle of it."

He hung up the phone as he joined the others. "FBI are on their way, along with local police. My mom diverted her plane; they should be here in thirty to forty minutes."

The wounded pilot groaned again.

Charley pointed to the cockpit. "You might tell them to bring a doctor."

SEVENTEEN

2:18 P.M.

The Feds got there first, then came the local police, fire brigade, and paramedics. Greg was treated for his many cuts and bruises, Charley and Wade were checked for concussions, and the fire department had to use the jaws of life to extricate the injured pilot.

The kids were questioned again by Special Agent Hill and Special Agent Dale. This time they weren't separated. And Agent Hill seemed surprisingly chagrined.

"Sorry we didn't listen to you kids," Agent Hill said to Charley. "If we had, Alton Peck might not have gotten away."

"It was a long shot," Charley conceded.

"Besides," Wade said with a grin, "I wouldn't say he's *entirely* gotten away."

Everyone looked confused until Wade added, "Oona, you still have Charley's phone?"

"Yeah. Sure."

"Where am I?"

Oona looked confused for a minute, then she giggled. "Okay. You are currently at a truck stop in Kenosha, Wisconsin."

"Yeah, I'm completely lost," Greg said.

"You and me both," Special Agent Hill agreed.

"Oona's been tracking us on Charley's phone ever since we left the impound lot."

Charley snapped her fingers. "That's what you were doing with the duffel bag! You slipped your phone into it!"

Within minutes Special Agent Hill had the Wisconsin state police, the highway patrol, and the Kenosha municipal police department surround the Gas 'N Gulp truck stop just off I-94, where Alton Peck was, finally, taken into custody.

"They got him!" Agent Hill announced when the call came through.

There was lots of cheering and hugging, and Agent Dale even rushed out to get some celebratory doughnuts.

Just as Senator Zelzah's plane landed on the adjacent runway.

Senator Zelzah had Alton Peck brought back to Fox Lake; she didn't want to let him out of her sight until she could watch him safely locked away with her own eyes. Though he was shackled and chained, and surrounded by about twenty state and federal law enforcement agents, Charley still felt a nauseating anxiety when he was taken from the back of a police cruiser and brought before the senator.

But seeing him up close now, unarmed, Charley was overwhelmed with a feeling of, well, sadness. Not sadness *for* him really; what she felt was not pity. She knew that much. But sadness because of what he stood for.

Peck's life was supposed to be the dream. The biggest company, the most money, the coolest toys. He had it all, but deep down he didn't appreciate any of it. While everyone was waiting for the FBI, Greg had showed Charley and the others the hangar full of boats and cars and motorcycles and paintings and statues and rare antiquities, and they were just ... there. Taking up space. Acquired, but useless.

Charley remembered what Peck had said, screamed actually, right before grabbing the plane's controls and running over the Mustang. The car he'd supposedly bought to honor his late father.

I'll show you.

She knew, deep down, that he was talking to his dad, the memory of him. That he'd really bought the car to stick it to his dad, not to honor him. After Alton Peck was apprehended in Kenosha, Charley took her phone back and looked up Alton Peck's father. There wasn't much to find. His name was Thomas and he sold life insurance. He was well-liked and lived a quiet life. He wasn't rich, he wasn't powerful. He did all right.

So why did Alton Peck hate him so much?

I'll show you.

Maybe it was because of what his father had tried to show him when he dragged his young son to all those car shows. That you could appreciate something, love it even, without having to possess it. Thomas Peck loved cars, ones he knew he would never own. To his son, that made him a loser.

But Alton Peck, as brilliant as he was, had missed the point. So while he'd become one of the richest, most powerful men in the country, he was, perhaps, also the unhappiest.

As Agents Hill and Dale brought Peck to Senator Zelzah, she leaned over to Charley.

"Any parting shots before I take him away?"

Charley shook her head. "He wouldn't listen anyway."

"You sure you don't want a ride back to campus?" Senator Zelzah fussed over her son. "I can have one of the agents return the car to your fraternity brother for you."

"Ma, I got it," Oscar said, standing his ground.

The senator started to object, but then looked at her son carefully and backed off. "Okay," she said. "But text me the minute you're back on campus."

"I will, Ma."

"And the rest of you," Senator Zelzah said to Charley and the others. "I trust this time you will go home and stay there?"

"And keep quiet," Agent Hill said, with a little smile to Charley.

"And keep quiet," Senator Zelzah repeated.

Everyone nodded solemnly. Then Greg led the group back to the car, where Wade practically threw himself on the hood of the Mustang. "Oh, you gave me such a scare."

"Would you two like a minute alone?" Charley quipped.

"Maybe."

"Come on," Greg said, ushering them into the car. "Charley and I still need to straighten up the house before Mom and Derrick get back."

"How much time do you have?" Oona asked.

"They're due to land in an hour," Greg said. "Probably gives us two before they're back at the house."

They got in and Greg started up the car. "Everybody buck-led?" he said. "Let's go home."

The house was in pretty good shape, probably because they hadn't really been in it all night. The dishwasher needed to be unloaded, some wayward clothes were tossed into hampers, but otherwise, they were golden.

"Well," Wade said after throwing an old pizza box in the recycling bin. "I think I'll go home and give my parents a piece of my mind about their joint-custody arrangement."

"Really?" Charley said, surprised.

"Yeah, well. Sometimes you have to say the hard things. Especially to people you care about." He shot Oona a quick glance. "A friend of mine taught me that."

Charley couldn't be sure, but for a second there it looked like Oona was at a complete loss for words. But just for a second.

"I should probably head home as well," Oona said, clearing her throat. "Though I think I'll go easy on my parents. They deserve a break."

"Don't forget your phone," Charley said on their way out.

"Oh, right," Oona laughed, grabbing her cell phone off the end table.

After they left, Greg came downstairs.

"Mom just texted," he said. "She and Derrick landed at O'Hare. Between baggage claim and traffic, they'll probably be home in about an hour."

Charley looked her brother over. His left arm was looking pretty gnarly. The road rash from his dive on the runway was starting to bruise purple and yellow.

"What are we going to tell them about that?" she said, pointing to his injuries.

He shrugged. "That I took a bad slide into second."

Charley shook her head. "You are a bad slide into second."

Greg gave a confused guffaw. "What does that even mean?"

"I don't know," Charley laughed. "But it fits."

"It kind of does."

"Hey. Thanks for getting run over by a plane for me."

"Anytime."

Charley and Greg shared that awkward moment when hugs and I-love-yous hover in the air between a brother and sister but never (to the silent relief of both parties) quite materialize.

Greg bit his top lip and started to fidget with his hands. Charley could see it clearly now, what Marisa had been talking about before. He needed to move, move, move. But everything had finally stopped, and Greg was getting squirrelly. His eyes kept drifting toward the front door.

He's going to run, Charley thought. *He's going to come up with some errand to distract himself.* It didn't make her mad, though. *If it's what he needs*, she thought, *let him go.*

Greg took a long, deep breath. "So," he said. "Want to put on one of those movies?"

"It's cool," Charley said. "I can—wait, what?"

"We never got our movie night." Greg shrugged. "I thought maybe we could at least start one before Mom and Derrick get back. Whaddya say?"

Charley said, "Sure. I'd like that."

They put on *Hot Fuzz*. He made it about ten minutes before he fell asleep.

Charley looked over at her brother, completely passed out on the long side of the sectional, and smiled to herself. Then she got up to take some recycling to the trash bins in the garage. On her way back inside, she stopped to look at the Mustang, parked carefully in the exact same place Derrick left it a week ago, and smiled to herself.

It had all worked out. Everything was, miraculously, okay.

The minute the thought popped into her mind, two others chased right after.

The first thought was, *Don't jinx it, stupid.*

The second thought was, *Wait, what's that?*

Charley ran over to the Mustang, hoping against hope that it was just some trick of the light. But up close there was no mistaking it.

A small but undeniable scratch just above the back bumper.

And that's when her mom's car pulled into the driveway.

Her mom honked enthusiastically, and Charley spun around, pressing her back up against the car to hide the scratch.

Greg came out to meet them and help bring in the luggage. Fortunately for Charley, her mom was so glad to see her that she didn't notice her daughter hadn't moved from her spot in front of the Mustang.

"You okay?" her mom asked after a long, tight hug.

"Yeah, yeah," Charley said halfheartedly. "I just didn't get much sleep last night."

Charley followed everyone else into the house. Derrick hadn't noticed the scratch, hadn't even given his car a second look. But Charley felt no relief. It was just a matter of time.

They dropped the luggage in the mudroom, then Mom herded Charley and Greg into the family room.

"Guys," she said, bubbling with excitement. "Derrick and I have something to tell you. We're getting married!"

"No way!" Greg laughed, hugging Mom, and then Derrick. "Congratulations!"

Their mom quickly launched into the story of how Derrick proposed. It was by a lagoon and not on a volcano, but Charley had to admit it sounded every bit as magical and romantic. Not that either of those things really interested her. But credit where it's due and all that.

Then Greg shared his news about the University of British Columbia, which led to a whole other round of cheers and tears and hugs. Charley's mom didn't notice how Charley had been quietly keeping her distance from the whole celebration.

Derrick noticed, though.

Charley knew what she had to do, and the sooner the better. She went over to Derrick and said quietly, "Can we talk outside for a minute?"

"Um, sure," Derrick said, sharing a confused look with Charley's mom. Greg was also confused, but that was why Charley knew she had to act fast.

She led Derrick out through the garage and showed him the scratch on the Mustang.

"It's my fault," she said quickly. "I did it on Friday. I was riding my bike and I came into the garage too fast and scraped the handle bar on the back of your car. I'm sorry."

Derrick gave her a curious look. Then he said, "No, you didn't."

"What?"

"Charley, I got that scratch two weeks ago."

"You did?"

"Uh-huh. At the supermarket. Runaway shopping cart, most likely."

"Oh," Charley said as her mind scrambled for the best way to pivot out of her lie. "I . . . I . . ."

"It's okay," Derrick said. He looked more amused than upset, but Charley wasn't sure that was necessarily better.

She started to tear up, which made her feel ridiculous. Puka Necklace (aka Dirk, aka Dirk the Jerk) and the convenience store aggro-bros never made her cry. The Woznikowski brothers never made her cry. Even a gun-toting Alton Peck couldn't make her cry. But her mom's boyfriend (scratch that, fiancé) was bringing her to tears and he wasn't even trying. How lame was that?

"Hey, hey," Derrick said consolingly. Then, seeing that wasn't helping, he changed tactics. "All right, Charley. I'm going to go out on a limb here. What I'm guessing happened is that your brother took the car out sometime while your mom and I were in Hawaii, and that you think he scratched the car, so you made up this story to protect him."

Close enough, Charley thought.

"In which case," Derrick continued, "I'm impressed."

"What?"

"Taking the fall for your brother. Lying to protect him. I really respect that. But even if your brother *had* scratched the car, you don't need to lie to me about it."

"Nah, I'm sorry. I don't buy it," she said, wiping her nose on her sleeve. "You love that car. It's a classic."

"I do. And it is," he conceded. "But at the end of the day, it's just a milkshake."

Charley stopped. "What did you just say?"

"I said it's just a Mustang," Derrick repeated.

"Oh," Charley said. "Right."

"And if we're being honest, it's not even one of the best ones. It's not a Shelby, or the Steve McQueen Mustang. It's just really rare. But that's not why I love it. The reason it means so much to me is that it meant so much to my uncle. Some of my happiest memories are the times he took me driving in it. And I want that for you and Greg, too. To create your own memories with that car."

Well, no worries there, Charley thought.

"And if that means getting a ding or a scratch or whatever, then big deal."

"But you told Greg he wasn't allowed to drive it while you guys were gone."

"That's right. Because he isn't insured on it. But as soon as your mom and I are on the same car insurance, he can drive it whenever he wants. Same goes for you, once you get your license."

"Really?"

"Of course," Derrick said.

Suddenly, inexplicably, all Charley could think about right now was Alton Peck. Not like he is now, but when he was a kid, at the car shows with his dad. Because like Peck, Charley was being shown something right now and she didn't want to miss it. What Derrick was saying was that the joy in having anything came from sharing it with people you cared about. Otherwise, what was the point?

"Thanks, Derrick," Charley said.

"Who wants takeout for dinner tonight?" Derrick announced as he and Charley came back in the house.

Greg shot Charley a questioning look. Their mom threw one Derrick's way as well. Charley gave her brother a tight, all clear nod of the head.

Then Greg said, "So, Mom. You were asking about how I got all banged up?"

"Oh, right," she answered. "Sliding into second?"

"Yeah. Funny thing, it's kind of a blur. Charley, you were there."

"I was? I mean, yeah. I was there."

"Do you remember how it went down?"

Charley smiled and bit her cheek. So he wanted to play the line game, did he? "Well, it happened in the fifth inning. But it really all started in the second. See, Greg was getting mouthy with the first baseman from the other team. Big guy, barbwire tattoos on his arms."

"Ugh," Derrick laughed. "Barbwire?"

"He was a growler, too," Greg added. "No, seriously. He literally growled, real low, every time I stepped off the bag. I thought he was going to bite my ankle if I tried to steal second."

"Oh, my word," their mom said.

Greg smiled his shortstop smile. In a few months, that smile would be all the way in Canada. Charley was going to miss that smile. But it was here now.

And it was her turn.

"And don't forget about the puka shell necklace," Charley said.

"Ha!" Greg exclaimed. "That's right! How could I forget about the necklace?"

"No way," Derrick laughed.

"Honest to god," Charley said. "Anyway, it's the top of the second. And Greg keeps going on and on about how cool he thinks that necklace is. Where did he get it? How long has he had it? Really getting under the guy's skin. But Greg just keeps at it, keeps making small talk. Asking him how school's going, what his plans are for the summer. What he thinks of the Marvel Phase Four rollout. And it's just making this guy madder and madder until finally . . ."

ACKNOWLEDGMENTS

No one does it alone. At least no one I've ever met.

Thanks to my family, for their support and patience. And encouragement. And patience, because that one bears repeating.

Thanks to Lena, for helping me get those early chapters just right.

Thank you, Emily Mitchell, for being such an amazing agent, in all kinds of weather.

Even four years later, I remain awestruck with gratitude for my editor, Jenne Abramowitz, who only ever wants the best for her writers. I continue to learn so much from working with you.

Thanks to Stephanie Yang, Yaffa Jaskoll, Janell Harris, Rachel Feld, Julia Eisler, Elisabeth Ferrari, and the whole brilliant, tireless Scholastic family. It's such a privilege to work with people who are so kind, wise, and passionate about what they do.

And, finally, thank you, Kirsten. For everything.

ABOUT THE AUTHOR

Keith Calabrese is the author of *A Drop of Hope* and *Connect the Dots*. He lives in Los Angeles with his wife, kids, and a dog who thinks he's a mountain goat.